"I LONG TO LOVE YOU—NOW."

Patrick's voice was a tender whisper, a poignant line of poetry from a love scene she had never heard before. A sense of dizziness left Vicky swaying backward, and she found herself half reclining on the sofa, Patrick's body insistent against hers.

Slowly, his hands began to unbutton her dress, while she responded with a throb of desire that emanated from the very center of her being. She wondered for a dazed moment if she were playing a role before an audience which she could not see. But no, the fine blue garments which Patrick removed from her body were not a costume. They belonged to her, to Vickey Owens, not an actress, but a real woman who was being heated by a passion more intense than she had ever felt before. And still it mounted, raging into a thousand flames she was helpless to extinguish while she whispered, "Yes, Patrick, yes. . . ."

ROSALYNN CARROLL is an unabashed romantic who finds avenues for creative expression in both fiction writing and the theater. Married for a long and happy time, Ms. Carroll enjoys traveling with her husband to explore settings for the unwritten stories that are always simmering in her mind. She lives in Ann Arbor, Michigan.

Dear Reader:

We at Rapture Romance hope you will continue to enjoy our four books each month as much as we enjoy bringing them to you. Our commitment remains strong to giving you only the best, by well-known favorite authors and exciting new writers.

We've used the comments and opinions we've heard from *you*, the reader, to make our selections, so please keep writing to us. Your letters have already helped us bring you better books—the kind you want—and we appreciate and depend on them. Of course, we are always happy to forward mail to our authors—writers need to hear from their fans!

And don't miss any of the inside story on Rapture. To tell you about upcoming books, introduce you to the authors, and give you a behind-the-scenes look at romance publishing, we've started a *free* newsletter, *The Rapture Reader*. Just write to the address below, and we will be happy to send you each issue.

Happy reading!

The Editors
Rapture Romance
New American Library
1633 Broadway
New York, NY 10019

ENCHANTED ENCORE

by

Rosalynn Carroll

RAPTURE ROMANCE

NEW AMERICAN LIBRARY

PUBLISHER'S NOTE

This novel is a work of fiction. Names, characters, places, and incidents either are the product of the author's imagination or are used fictitiously, and any resemblance to actual persons, living or dead, events, or locales is entirely coincidental.

NAL BOOKS ARE AVAILABLE AT QUANTITY DISCOUNTS
WHEN USED TO PROMOTE PRODUCTS OR SERVICES.
FOR INFORMATION PLEASE WRITE TO PREMIUM MARKETING DIVISION,
NEW AMERICAN LIBRARY, 1633 BROADWAY,
NEW YORK, NEW YORK 10019.

Copyright © 1984 by Carol Katz

SIGNET, SIGNET CLASSIC, MENTOR, PLUME, MERIDIAN and NAL BOOKS
are published by New American Library,
1633 Broadway, New York, New York 10019

First Printing, May, 1984

1 2 3 4 5 6 7 8 9

PRINTED IN THE UNITED STATES OF AMERICA

For Gene,
whose gift of love is the source
of every word I write

Chapter One

Vicky Owens got ready for her early-morning meeting in her usual rush. Being the costume designer for the theater department of the local university seemed to leave her little enough time for elaborate attention to her own wardrobe and personal appearance. Still, a quick glance in the bathroom mirror told her she looked just fine. Her dark eyes sparkled from a sound night's sleep, and after a quick brushing her short black hair fell obediently into place like a glossy cap upon her head. She noticed a few new gray hairs, and she wondered again if she should finally submit to dying it. No, that would somehow be dishonest, not her style at all. Besides, by the time you reached the age of thirty-six you were entitled to a few gray strands as a sign of your wisdom and maturity. Vicky smiled at herself before she touched her mouth lightly with lipstick. On this April morning in Ann Arbor, the forsythia bush outside her window was dazzling her eye with brilliant yellow blossoms, and she hardly felt much older than her fifteen-year-old daughter, Bethanne.

"Mom, I've gotta dash. I'm sorry I took so long in the bathroom, but Bud will be picking me up in his new car in just a sec." A breathless Bethanne, fresh from a long session with her blow drier and curling iron, kissed her mother hastily on the cheek. "Oh, I might be a little late this afternoon. Bud wants me to help him after school with a term paper."

Vicky paused briefly, trying to find a tactful way to phrase her thoughts. Being the single parent of an emotional teenager wasn't easy, and for a moment she thought fondly of George. He would have known just how to handle this situation. There was no doubt that Bethanne needed a firm male hand for guidance, but Vicky, a widow these past two years, was entirely on her own.

"Bethanne, you know how much I like Bud. He's polite and responsible, and I have nothing but praise for a high school senior who can save up enough money from a part-time job to buy himself a car. But ... well, don't you think you might be seeing too much of each other? He seems to be taking the place of just about everything else in your life. Your music lessons, for instance. I don't believe you've practiced in over a week."

Bethanne bit her lip. She was a slender, dark-haired girl who had only recently emerged from leggy awkwardness into a state of budding young womanhood. "Oh, Mom, I know, and I'm sorry. I'll try to practice more, I promise." She hugged her schoolbooks to her chest impulsively. "It's just that . . . oh, I don't know—maybe it's just spring fever. You know what I mean, don't you?"

Vicky smiled with understanding. She knew very well what Bethanne meant, but she still felt that her words of advice should make an impact. "There's no reason why you can't see Bud as well as continue to play the harp," she suggested firmly. "There's room enough in your life for both things, Bethanne. All it takes is some thoughtful planning on your part."

"I'll practice all night, I promise," the girl vowed with heartfelt earnestness. Then she laughed exuberantly, spinning herself around in a full circle. "But, Mom, don't you remember what it was like to be young and in love for the first time and all bubbly inside? I know you loved Daddy, but wasn't there anyone who ever made you feel sort of magical?"

The scent of lilacs floated bewitchingly through the window, and suddenly Vicky remembered as if it were only yesterday how she and Patrick Wallingford had strolled, hand in hand, through the streets of London. But that had been . . . how long ago? A full eighteen years. She was surprised that the memory had come back to her with such vivid clarity.

"I remember," she mused softly, her dark eyes glistening against the fair translucence of her skin. "It was when I was in London studying at the Royal Academy of Dramatic Arts. I've told you about my time there. The young man was an actor—a very gifted one, too."

"Oh, Mom, tell me more," Bethanne pleaded with delight.

"Well, there's really not a whole lot to tell," Vicky replied with deliberate vagueness, reluctant to share all the details with her daughter. "We spent a lovely summer together, and when it was over we simply went our separate ways."

"But why, Mom? If he was an actor, I'll bet he was handsome."

"Very," said Vicky softly as his image appeared clearly in her mind's eye. With his thick golden hair and those compelling blue eyes set in a face that was lean and boldly chiseled, he had been extremely handsome. But Patrick had possessed more than just good looks. There had been a certain magnetism about him, a kind of dynamic intensity in his bearing and demeanor that had made people stop and turn their heads whenever he passed their way. Yes, Patrick Wallingford had been a man with a commanding presence both on the stage and off; one strong enough to return to Vicky's memory like a sudden electrical current.

"But, Mom, what happened?" Bethanne was persisting, wide-eyed and eager to hear more of the story.

Vicky reached out and playfully rumpled her daughter's hair. "What usually happens with most starry-eyed romances, young lady. It just came to an end. When the summer was over we said good-bye and I . . . I returned home to my own normal world."

A horn sounded from outside, causing Bethanne to respond instantly. "There's Bud now," she exclaimed as she dashed down the hall. Then she stopped abruptly and called back. "Oh, we'll be driving by campus, so we can drop you off if you like."

But Vicky wanted to be outside and enjoy the sweetness of the spring air. The campus was less than a mile away, and she liked to walk there along shady streets and rows of quaint Victorian houses whenever she could. Besides, walking was good exercise and a pleasant way to maintain her figure, which was as trim as it had been in London some eighteen years ago.

She quickly gathered the papers she would need for her meeting, glancing back at the house with a small surge of satisfaction. Like many others in Ann Arbor, it had a turn-of-the-century charm with its high-ceilinged rooms and generous woodwork, stained to a dark, mellow glow under the persistent efforts of her own hands. It wasn't a large or imposing house, but it had been home to her for almost seventeen years, and she had done her best to fill it with warm colors and a pleasant sense of nostalgia.

Last night's rain had deepened the color of the trees and lawns along Olivia Street to a

glowing shade of emerald. Vicky turned a corner in the direction of the campus. As ever, the
coming of spring was a miracle she fully savored,
especially in Michigan, where the winters were
long and punishing. Soon she became part of
the promenade of strollers, most of whom were
students coming from nearby rooming houses.
Many of them were couples, holding hands and
laughing softly in the throes of fresh young love.

Vicky smiled with recognition. Such signs of
courtship were as much a part of springtime as
the pink blossoms sprinkled over the dogwood
trees. She loved all the different seasons, but
this one, with all its sweet promise of new life to
come, was the one she loved best of all.

Her own special season of first love had certainly seemed to promise everything. And why
not? Her head had been filled with wonderful
illusions, and at the age of eighteen she had
been sure that her dream of becoming a celebrated actress—a great lady of the stage—was
only a few years away. Whom better to share
the dream with than Patrick Wallingford? At
the time, he was a penniless young theater
student, but he would not, it had seemed, remain so for long. As he squired her about the
narrow lanes and cobbled streets of old London,
he had talked with such knowing wit and keen
intellect about his plans that Vicky had no doubt
that his own dreams would eventually come true.
In classes at the academy he outshone all the
others, not with arrogance but with an intensity

of feeling and a sure sense of the stage that seemed to emanate from deep within him. Even then he had possessed an extraordinary larger-than-life quality. As Vicky had watched him with awe and adoration she knew beyond a doubt that he was marked for great accomplishments.

It had hardly been a surprise when he landed a job with a small repertory company at the end of the summer—a promising beginning to his career. But when Vicky had auditioned for a role in the same company, she was passed over for an actress with far more ability. It had come as a rude blow at the time, but it confirmed what she had already begun to sense: as a performer she was only mediocre, and with her merely pleasant appearance she didn't stand a chance against truly gifted actresses with striking beauty.

She had returned to the States, saddened but wiser. She was simply not meant to share a theatrical life in London with Patrick, and there was no sense in deluding herself. Besides, there was someone at home who was a far more realistic prospect for her—George Owens, a university professor, who had been patiently waiting until she came back down to earth. She had married him within six months of her return, a decision she had never regretted. George had been steady, thoughtful, and kind, and the twenty-one-year age difference between them had only enhanced their relationship. In some ways George had been a father figure to Vicky, and because she had grown up without a father of her own, she had welcomed her husband's gentle protectiveness, especially in the early years of their marriage.

Vicky approached the heart of the University of Michigan campus at State Street, where she stopped for a red light. Yes, her quiet, secure life with George had suited her well. She had been able to combine her love for the theater and her eye for design into working with costumes right here in Ann Arbor at a job she adored. She had made her choice years ago, and it had steered her along a path that was still richly satisfying.

She crossed the street in a jumble of blue-jeaned students and professors with briefcases. Just across from her was the Diag, a shady lawn crisscrossed with walkways running diagonally from each corner and meeting in the center at the library. Vicky headed for the white-columned, graceful Angell Hall, where the meeting was to be held. The campus was lovely, especially in spring, and she impulsively plucked a tempting pink flower from a nearby cherry tree. She was glad to have made her life in this peaceful place. It was a life far different from that of Patrick Wallingford, who, from what she knew, busily divided his time between the glittering theatrical worlds of London and New York. He had made his mark in his inimitable style, after all, to become one of the most acclaimed directors of the modern stage. He had, of course, been destined for such a life, Vicky surmised, while she had found happiness in a quieter way. A picture of him, more vivid than ever, shot through her memory, but she pushed it away. Things had a way of working out for the best. Surely it was only spring fever that made her think of him at all.

She walked into the meeting room, where the familiar members of the theater faculty were helping themselves to cups of coffee. She nodded pleasantly to them as she took her place at the long table. Benson Barnett, the head of the department, was already seated and pulling out a batch of papers from his briefcase in the manner of a jolly, academic Santa Claus, about to present a series of goodies to his faculty members.

Vicky nodded at him, wondering why his full cheeks were so florid and why his bespectacled eyes twinkled with more than their usual share of merriment. He was probably looking forward to the upcoming production of *Cyrano de Bergerac*, she concluded, which he was slated to direct. Benson's administrative duties normally didn't permit him such colorful assignments, but he had taken this one on quite willingly when previous plans for a visiting director had fallen through. He winked at her good-naturedly, and she smiled back. In many ways the widowed Benson qualified more closely than anyone else since George's death to being Vicky's boyfriend— that is, if she could consider his invitations to lunch and coffee as dates. But the fact of the matter was that she didn't. Benson was a friend to everyone, and his door was always open to faculty and students alike. Vicky respected the genial way he ran the department and his ability to see that all ran smoothly. Somehow, though, she could never consider him as anything more than a kindly colleague.

Benson started the meeting by elaborating on tedious, routine items while Vicky doodled languidly. This matter-of-fact business couldn't be the reason he had called this meeting, and she wished he would get to the point. Outside the window Vicky could see students frolicking with a Frisbee under the boughs of a leafy tree, and she sighed. Benson had a tendency to be verbose. She hoped he would not drone on for too long.

When he straightened the perky bow tie above his bright red sweater and cleared his throat rather loudly, Vicky came to attention. He was about to make an announcement of some kind. She raised her head with interest.

"Ahem," Benson said again for effect, his bright eyes roving the room to see that all the faculty members were alert and attentive. "I know you've all been wondering why I've called this special meeting, and I assure you that what I'm about to tell you will not be disappointing. It concerns a change in our plans for *Cyrano de Bergerac*. It looks as as though yours truly"—he bowed his head modestly—"will be taking a back seat in the production, after all. I'm enormously proud to announce that I've been able to secure the talents of none other than the distinguished Patrick Wallingford. He has graciously consented to fly in from New York to fill the position of visiting director."

Low murmurs of appreciation were heard from everyone around the table—except from Vicky, who remained silent, her fair skin turning even whiter against the darkness of her hair.

Benson smilingly held his hand up in order to be heard above the buzzing voices. "Not only will our department be able to boast of one distinguished theatrical celebrity, but we will, it seems, be honored by yet another. Diana Galloway, one of the leading ladies of the stage, will be joining Wallingford to take the female lead in the production. I understand that since their divorce they have maintained an—er—a sort of working relationship. I'm not aware of all the whys and wherefores, and I certainly didn't wish to pry. All I know is that one absolutely refused to come to Ann Arbor without the other."

Vicky's heart was thumping wildly in her chest, but she purposely kept her eyes glued to the papers before her. She was aware that the other faculty members were all exchanging looks of wide-eyed interest at this rather amazing bit of news. At one end of the table Leroy Leonard, the department's set designer, who had spent several years in New York, grimaced good-naturedly.

"Congratulations, Benson," he said. "You've outdone yourself this time, but I should warn you to expect some fireworks. From what I've heard, Wallingford and his ex-wife have a tendency to go at it tooth and nail when they're together." This comment was greeted with wry chuckles.

"Now, now," Benson counseled in a calming voice, "let's not allow ourselves to be influenced by mere hearsay. Besides, the presence of these two outstanding talents will be a credit to the department. If our guests wish to use Ann Arbor as the scene for a marital reunion, we should consider ourselves most fortunate, indeed."

The trembling of Vicky's hands caused some of her papers to flutter to the floor. She bent to retrieve them, embarrassed to see that her jumpy reaction was drawing mildly curious looks from everyone around her.

She was thankful that the group was far more interested in Benson's news than in her temporary case of the jitters, and their eyes passed over her quickly.

"Benson, I'm delighted to hear that Wallingford will be directing the production," remarked Joan Armbruster, who taught voice and diction. "I've admired his ability for years, and I'm sure that working with him will be a creative challenge. But Galloway . . . well, I must confess that I'm somewhat surprised about her. To my knowledge she hasn't worked steadily for several seasons. Besides"—her well-modulated voice took on the slightest edge of cattiness—"isn't she a wee bit old to be playing the role of Roxane?"

Benson, as adept as ever in placating occasional dissent from members of the faculty, nodded understandingly to Joan. "I appreciate your concerns, of course," he told her with a cherubic smile on his rosy face. "Rest assured that Miss Galloway is a professional actress of the highest caliber, as well as a lady of exceptional beauty. I have no doubt that she'll come through splendidly. Naturally, proper makeup and costuming will be essential to the production, but we have nothing to worry about on that score. Vicky Owens has just completed a series of excellent costume designs under my supervision, and she'll continue to put her best efforts into the production once it gets under way."

He nodded encouragingly at Vicky, and she smiled back mutely, not trusting herself to speak in a rational manner. Yes, she would be working as the costumer for the show, but until now she'd had no idea that her responsibilities would have to be performed in the disturbing presence of her old flame and his ex-wife. It promised to be an unsettling experience at best, and her still-trembling hands grew clammy at the very prospect.

Benson, satisfied that he had successfully quelled all doubt, settled back, locking his pink hands across the expanse of his sturdy chest. "I know all of you will do your level best to welcome our two visiting artists to Ann Arbor. I will be acting as assistant director of the play—to see that everything goes off without a hitch. I urge the rest of you to follow my example so that our distinguished guests will feel entirely comfortable. This will be a team effort, after all, and we'll want to give it our best."

The rest of the meeting passed in a blur before Vicky's eyes. She knew only that a man whom she'd tried to leave forever in London would be invading her tranquil life in less than a week's time. What might come of such an uneasy reunion she didn't know, but her life, for the duration of Wallingford's stay, would be anything but tranquil. She tried to tell herself that her breathless reactions were as adolescent as those of her daughter, Bethanne; even so, her heart continued its frantic pace while strange little sparks darted through her body to the very tips of her fingers and toes.

"How about a cup of coffee, Vicky?" Benson asked after the meeting had ended. "You look as if you could use a snappy little pick-me-up." He was peering into her pale face with a look of friendly concern.

She tried her best to smile. "Thanks, Benson, but I . . . I've got some errands to run. I really should be on my way." Actually, the time ahead of her was entirely free, but she did not wish to spend it with Benson, who would be sure to make jolly references to the fact that he had secured the coveted services of someone like Patrick Wallingford for the undeniable glory and prestige of his department.

She felt Benson's hand patting her shoulder in a reassuring manner. "Vicky, my dear, you don't have a thing to worry about. You do your job beautifully, and I'm sure that your costume designs will meet with full approval, even from a man as exacting as Patrick Wallingford." He wagged his finger before her playfully. "I'm counting on you to see the production through with your usual excellence and vigor."

"Will do, Benson," she responded in a deliberately casual tone of voice as she pretended to be unconcerned. There was certainly no reason for her to divulge an eighteen-year-old secret of the heart to anyone, including the kindly Benson Barnett. Receptive to hearing the occasional confidences of the faculty, he fully enjoyed the role of a wise and paternalistic counselor, but this was one confidence he was not going to hear.

Vicky was soon on her way back home, her taut nerves relaxing somewhat during her walk. Clusters of tulips in bold yellows, reds and purples waved their cupped heads in the mid-morning breeze, and the air was filled with the chirping of birds, newly returned from southern climates and busily engaged in nest-building. She took a deep breath before she smiled a little at her foolish apprehensions.

It had been eighteen years since she had seen Patrick Wallingford, and in the passage of time many things had changed. She, for one, was no longer the starry-eyed dreamer she had been in London. And he, she assumed, had also changed. Perhaps he had become paunchy and unappealing over the years, enough so that he would no longer have the devastating effect she remembered so well. All things were possible. She could only hope against hope and brace herself for their inevitable meeting.

Chapter Two

❧

What to wear when meeting the man who had captured your heart years ago? Vicky considered the clothes in her closet with her costume designer's eye. If she were a character in a play, she might choose a flowery dress flounced with girlish ruffles to convey the image of eternal youth. She chuckled softly to herself. Such illusions didn't suit her at all. She would simply be herself, she thought as she donned a pair of beige slacks, a plum-colored shirt, and a mandarin-style jacket. When she checked in the mirror, she saw no miraculous transformation. Just the pleasant, dark-eyed face of a woman who lived a serene life and did not regret it. And that, she realized, as she wondered again how the passage of time had affected Patrick Wallingford, was exactly what she was.

Vicky approached the Lydia Mendelssohn Theater an hour later with her costume sketches tucked securely in her portfolio. The theater itself, an ivy-covered Gothic-revival building of red brick, had an air of antique gentility about it that Vicky had always loved. Several years ago there had been talk of tearing it down because of its rather venerable age, especially in this day of cold, contemporary structures of glass and steel. A number of local admirers, Vicky included, had fought to preserve it, however, and as a result the Lydia remained on campus, a charming reminder of a bygone era.

But the warm familiarity of this theater, in which Vicky had so often worked, did little to calm her jittery anticipation. In a short while she would be face to face with Patrick Wallingford, not as the girl she had once been but as the experienced costumer for this new production. Her heart kept a rapid tempo as she quietly stole inside the auditorium. Wallingford was conducting tryouts for the play this afternoon. Although the role of Roxane had been filled by his ex-wife, Diana Galloway, the other parts would all be given to talented university students.

The stage was softly lit and occupied by several young actors with scripts in their hands. The auditorium, however, was dark, in contrast to the bright spring sunshine outside. Vicky leaned against the wall by the front exit, hugging her portfolio to her chest as her eyes adjusted to the dim surroundings. She felt safe and anonymous here, and she waited rather tremulously for what was to come.

One of the actors on stage was a graduate student named David Lang. Vicky knew he had his heart set on the coveted role of Cyrano de Bergerac, and she listened as he read aloud. His monologue was one of the play's most romantic passages, but David, who usually read quite well, was handling the lines with stilted awkwardness.

When he finished, he peered questioningly into the audience and began to address his words to someone seated there.

"For some reason that speech has been giving me a hard time," he confessed with a little laugh. "I guess I'm afraid of overdoing it or somthing. It . . . it seems a little heavy."

"That's only because you're interpreting it with a twentieth-century mind," came a forceful, resonant voice from somewhere in the auditorium. "What you must do is take yourself into the world of romantic illusion, where men are willing to sacrifice themselves bravely on the altar of love, even dying for it, if need be."

Vicky turned her head in the direction of the speaker. The rich, deep voice rang effortlessly with precise British clarity through the auditorium. The speaker could only be Patrick Wallingford. The flow of words continued, brilliantly penetrating the heart of his subject just as Vicky remembered.

"I confess that such romantic ideals have been lost in this day and age," he went on with a note of wry amusement, "but as an actor it is up to you to bring them back to life. You must let yourself believe in them completely, and when you do, your audience will also believe with all of its heart."

The young actor nodded his head with understanding before he began to read again, but with much the same self-consciousness as he had shown before. Suddenly he stopped midway through the passage and shrugged sheepishly. "I don't think I'm getting it at all," he admitted lamely.

Vicky saw a tall, shadowy form rise from a row of seats ahead of her. "Well, it's not an easy thing to do," that resonant voice admitted in a crisp, reassuring tone. "I've had a bit of experience with it, so perhaps you'll let me show you what I have in mind."

He purposefully strode down a carpeted aisle to the stage. Instead of ascending by the small flight of steps on the side, he reached out and, using his arm as a pivot, vaulted with the lithe grace of an athlete up to the stage. In one firm, fluid movement he was standing, his body gliding to center stage with such swift sureness that he commanded the instant attention of everyone around him.

Vicky watched him with her heart in her mouth, her eyes drinking in every detail of his form and face. Patrick was the same as she remembered, she thought with a pang, yet different, too. His thick golden hair still crowned his head, but it was now mixed with gleaming strands of silver. Dressed in a pair of faded jeans, a black turtleneck sweater, and a tweed sport jacket with suede patches on the elbows, he was as lean and broad shouldered as ever. His springy step spoke of an undeniable fitness that had been well maintained over the years. His face was still handsome, and his eyes were still fired with a blazing intensity—but it was no longer the face of a young man; it reflected the seasons of experience he had weathered, only to become stronger than ever before.

She watched him without blinking as the two young actors moved downstage to make room. Yes, Patrick Wallingford had aged in the past eighteen years, but not the way she had hoped. He stood in the center of the stage and the lights from above cast a bewitching gleam of silver and gold upon his hair. Vicky knew beyond a doubt that she would live the weeks ahead of her in a state of uneasy turmoil. It was crazy, of course, to be at the mercy of such school-girl emotions. She had graduated into maturity years ago, so why was she now overcome by irrational feelings that she should have outgrown in adolescence?

Patrick was smiling slightly at the scattered members of his audience, most of them hopeful students who were auditioning for parts. He beckoned to them with beguiling words as he illuminated the message of the play for their benefit. "*Cyrano* is an unabashedly romantic work of art, conceived in the grandest tradition of courtly love. If it is to have meaning for the modern audience, we must allow ourselves to believe in it fully and without any reservations. See it as a kind of haunting legend, if you will, one that appeals to the romantic nature in all of us, one that we can rarely reveal to others." He paused, cutting a tall, striking figure as he thoughtfully began to stride downstage.

"In this particular passage we see the essence of the play itself. Here Cyrano speaks to the woman he truly loves, but he stands hidden in darkness beneath her balcony. His words, of course, come from his heart, but they are torn with anguish, too, for he believes his love is hopeless and will never be returned."

He paused momentarily to reach deep within his powers of concentration. Then he fixed his eyes intensely on an invisible presence while he began to recite the lines from memory. His rich baritone voice was nothing less than melodic, filling the auditorium like a magnificent musical instrument that responded instantly to his command, while the clipped British elegance of his speech was overlaid with the intriguing, earthier tones of his native Ireland.

"The feeling that holds me in its merciless grip could be nothing else but love! It has all the terrible jealousy and somber violence of love, and all the unselfishness, too. How gladly I would give my happiness for the sake of yours, even without your knowledge . . ."

The words were so compelling and so filled with tender expression that his audience hung on his every word, watching in rapt silence. As he continued his declaration of love to that invisible presence onstage, Vicky lost her sense of time and place. The moment became a small eternity for her, and she knew only that love was worth every sacrifice. It was splendid, too, for all its bittersweet anguish.

"Are you beginning to understand now? Do you feel my soul rising to you in the darkness?"

All of his being and energy were focused on his performance. When Vicky saw tears glistening in Patrick's eyes before they began to run unchecked down his face, she somehow knew that he believed the words with all of his heart. Still, he continued to speak, his magnetic stage presence and his sense of absolute control as flawless as ever.

"For you are trembling, like one of the leaves in the dark foliage above me: I've felt the beloved tremor of your hand descending along the jasmine branches!"

The members of the audience remained in hushed silence before they finally struggled back to reality, finally aware that the brief performance had come to an end. Scattered sounds of appreciative applause sounded through the theater, but Vicky stood still. Although the stage was bare of scenery, and the actor before her was attired only in his street clothes, she knew, nevertheless, that she had just witnessed a rare moment of theatrical magic.

"Heaven protect me from a man like him. If

he ever comes near me, I swear I'll have no defenses against him at all." Vicky heard a breathless voice by her side, and she turned to see Nancy Foster, a student, who had apparently entered the auditorium a few minutes before.

"Oh, is that you, Mrs. Owens?" the girl asked with a little giggle. "I'm sorry, I . . . I thought it was someone else." She turned away, embarrassed. "I only meant that Mr. Wallingford is a wonderful actor. He's so convincing, don't you think?"

Vicky nodded with what she hoped would appear as a serene expression of her mature understanding. It would never do to have the students guess the extent of her own reaction. Besides, there was probably little enough real substance in it. She had worked in the theater long enough to know that it was only a world of illusion. Yes, fine actors had the power to cast a spell onstage, but offstage, in the hard glare of reality, things usually looked far different.

Patrick was engaged in a quiet conversation with David Lang, but he suddenly glanced at his wristwatch.

"We'll continue with the readings for another hour or so, and then we'll take a break," he announced crisply to the group at large; once more he was the efficient director in charge of the production. "At that time I'd like to see a Mrs. Owens about the costumes." His eyes keenly probed the darkness before him. "Are you out there, Mrs. Owens?"

Although a simple affirmative reply was all that was required, Vicky found herself temporarily speechless. Patrick, of course, had no idea yet that Mrs. Owens had once been the Victoria Moore of his youth. Well, he would soon find out, but she lacked the nerve to tell him just now.

"Mrs. Owens is right here," said Nancy Foster in a loud effort to be helpful.

The director nodded briskly, his eyes roving the darkness, unable to see Vicky clearly. "Well, that's fine," he said matter-of-factly. "Why don't we meet in the costume room in about an hour's time? We have a lot to go over, and I'd like to begin as soon as possible." Without waiting for a reply, he swung himself impatiently down from the stage. "All those actors who are reading for the part of Christian de Neuvillette, please take your places," he announced, striding through the shadowy auditorium and settling back into a seat.

His eyes were soon riveted on a new group of actors, and Vicky slipped quietly through the exit on her way to the costume room. The public was familiar only with the carpeted plushness of the auditorium and its richly paneled lobby, but underneath lay a subterranean world where the backstage work of the theater was carried out. She passed the Green Room, which functioned as a general meeting and reception area, then the makeup room with its long rows of mirrors and counters. She went farther down into the basement of the building, finally arriving at the costume room, a lone figure with quaking knees and a heart that absolutely refused to behave in normal fashion.

She was greeted by a riot of brilliant colors. Gowns, cloaks, and tunics in a variety of jewellike tones hung from the rack along the far wall. Resting on open shelves were hats from all periods of history, including a pointed jester's cap with morris bells, a warrior's shiny helmet, and the more elaborate hat of a French cavalier, complete with lavish feathers. There was a feeling of fantastic glitter and make-believe that rarely failed to beguile anyone who entered the room, including Vicky herself. She tried to survey the sights around her with a realistic eye, knowing full well that things in the theater were rarely what they seemed. That suit of armor in the corner was nothing more than papier-mâché, dyed with lead coloring and varnished over for the proper shine. And the king's crown near it had been similarly fashioned; its golden glow came from metallic paint, and its opulent rubies were only simulated ones that Vicky had found in a secondhand-jewelry shop.

She knew that the old maxim "All that glitters is not gold" was true of the costumes she created. Maybe it was true of Patrick Wallingford, too. Onstage he still had the power to dazzle her eye with theatrical illusion. But offstage? Perhaps he would be entirely different. She could only wait and find out.

She was soon joined by a number of students, her willing assistants for the upcoming production. They began to ask eager questions about the work ahead, which would be challenging, for *Cyrano de Bergerac* was a play with many characters, all of whom required elaborate costumes. Vicky explained the details as clearly as she could. She enjoyed working with students. Their dauntless enthusiasm often encouraged her, and the time passed quickly.

Her young assistants were about to leave when one of them caught sight of an especially striking tall medieval hat covered with a silken fabric of delicate blue.

"This is such a beautiful hat, Mrs. Owens," she crooned as she fingered its long veil. "Is this worn over the face or behind the head?"

Vicky reached for it impulsively. "Here, let me show you," she said delightedly, placing it on her own head. The yards of chiffon trailed down the back of her neck and fell to her shoulders like a pale cloud.

"Oh, it's lovely on you, Mrs. Owens, the girl exclaimed with a clap of her hands. "Just *look* at yourself."

Vicky stepped over to the mirror, a fanciful little smile playing across her lips. She had to admit that the color was becoming to her. The frosty blue tones and flashing spangles brought out the blue lights in her black hair, and the delicacy of the hat complemented her creamy complexion.

"We used this for a production last year," she explained for the girl's benefit. "The character who wore it was a lady-in-waiting at the king's royal court." She draped the frothy veil about her face, her dark eyes and lashes taking on a mysterious glow. "These veils were used in all sorts of ways—sometimes for the sake of modesty and sometimes for reasons of pure flirtation."

The girl surveyed her with a twinkling smile. "Oh, I get it, Mrs. Owens," she said with a slight giggle. "I guess those ladies-in-waiting didn't want to have to wait around too long."

They all burst into merry peals of laughter as Vicky continued to hold the veil across her face in a pleasant flight of fancy. That was the alluring thing about costumes; all it took was a few spangles and some yards of chiffon for you to be transported into another time and place momentarily able to become anyone your heart desired.

Suddenly she was aware of footsteps in the doorway and a strong male voice just a few feet away. "I'm here to see Mrs. Owens, the costumer."

Vicky's heart leaped to her mouth as she stood transfixed, unable to respond. "There she is, Mr. Wallingford," the girl replied in a tone of instant solemnity. Then she began elbowing her companion. "Come on, Cindy, we'd better get going."

The girls disappeared in a flurry while Vicky

met the eyes of Patrick Wallingford in a flurry of her own. His tall, well-shaped form was striding toward her, even as she kept the veil about her face, hiding behind the flimsy folds that had become her last refuge from him.

He wore an alert, businesslike expression that gradually changed into bemused tenderness as he came closer. "Victoria Moore," he murmured with an air of soft incredulity, a smile teasing about the corners of his mouth. "It is you, isn't it, beneath that veil?" He reached for it as if he were engaged in an intriguing little game and lightly pushed it away from her face. "Only now you're hiding behind a veil instead of a young girl's first blush of innocence. But you really haven't changed at all." His smile was coaxing, causing crinkly little laugh lines to appear around his eyes as he continued to regard her warmly.

For a second she gazed back with a look of wonderment. Up close his electrical presence seemed even more intense, and his eyes were so blue, so piercingly blue . . . Suddenly she heard herself laugh in a small burst of protest. "Oh, but I've changed a great deal, Patrick," she said breathlessly. "I . . . I'm not even Victoria Moore any longer. I'm Vicky Owens now, and it . . . it seems we'll be working together on this production."

He inhaled softly. "Life is full of strange surprises, isn't it?" he mused with a low chuckle. "And I thought I'd never see you again, especially after you married. How long has it been, Victoria?"

"Well, I—I married George almost seventeen years ago," she stammered.

Patrick cocked his head in a playful manner. "Tell me now, this husband of yours—has he loved you well?"

Vicky searched his face for signs of mockery, but she found only tender curiosity, mixed with a momentary look of fleeting sadness. But why? A busy and successful man like Patrick Wallingford was not apt to look back on the past with lingering sentimentality. "Yes," she heard herself say. "I've had a good life, Patrick."

"There was a time when I would have loved you, too, differently from your husband, perhaps, but just as well." He watched for her reaction with such keen intensity that Vicky suddenly felt exposed, uncovered. "You do remember, don't you?"

She averted her eyes from his penetrating gaze and briskly removed the veiled hat. The illusions of the theater were always beguiling, but surely it was high time to return to solid earth and the world of reality. "Maybe we should just leave the past behind us, Patrick. It's all over and done with anyway . . ." She glanced about her at the glimmering costumes she had created. "Actually, I'm much too busy with the present to have time for needless reminiscing."

Something came into his eyes that looked very much like pain, and she was sorry her words had sounded so unkind. Still, no real harm had been done, for in an instant he was fully composed, becoming the very model of smooth decorum. "Yes, it's always wise to live in the present—and necessary, too, I suppose." He paused discreetly. "Well, I certainly hope I'll have the pleasure of meeting your husband while I'm in town. I've had occasion to read some of his essays on Shakespeare and I found them quite illuminating."

Vicky nodded soundlessly. It wasn't entirely surprising that Patrick was familiar with George's work, for Patrick had always been a man of wide interests and curiosity, and George had been a scholar of some repute. But George was no longer alive, and now was surely time for her to inform Patrick of that fact. Although the words were on the tip of her tongue, she couldn't bring herself to speak them. As a widow she was more vulnerable to Patrick Wallingford, and it was all too tempting to take shelter in George's safe, paternalistic shadow.

Patrick checked his wristwatch, taking on a businesslike air. "Perhaps we'll have time to talk more later on. Now, I'm afraid, we have our work cut out for us. Besides, I'm way behind schedule. I'd like to see your costume sketches, if you don't mind. That very jovial gentleman— your department head, Benson Barnett—informed me that you had them ready."

Thankful for this new and impersonal turn in their conversation, Vicky quickly fetched her portfolio. There was a sense of forceful impatience in Patrick's manner that made her want to obey him without further ado. He unaffectedly conveyed the kind of brisk authority that made those about him respond with full cooperation.

Patrick began to examine her sketches with the sharp, quick eye of an expert. As his head bent in concentration, the strands of his thick hair gleamed with gold and silver highlights. Vicky waited with quiet pride until he had finished. She had worked hard on these designs and had won the praise of everyone who had seen them. Benson had been particularly enthusiastic, and she hoped that Patrick would be impressed as well.

But to her chagrin she saw that he was not. And to make matters even worse was the fact that he was taking no pains to mince words. "I'll be frank, Victoria," he said, his eyes as cool as a November morning sky. "There's no time to be otherwise. The truth of it is that these aren't what I had in mind at all." He closed the cover of her portfolio firmly.

"But what ... what do you mean?" she asked as a flush of color rose to her cheeks. "Benson Barnett and I spent a lot of time on these. And we took special pains to see that each design was historically accurate."

"Yes, I can see that," he replied wryly. "But that's not quite the point. *Cyrano* is a play of extravagant romance and lyrical feeling, not a historical documentary. It should be a feast of color and beauty to the eye—nothing less. You've used far too many browns and drab shades of tan, for example. With colors like these, the actors will barely be noticed against the set."

It had been Benson's idea to match the costumes almost exactly to the colors of the set, and although Vicky had originally expressed doubts about his somewhat cautious plans, she now felt called upon to defend him. "But Benson and I agreed upon the color scheme. You see, we wanted the costumes to complement the set, not to compete with it."

Patrick folded his arms against his chest, observing her indignation with a calm little smile. "But I've taken full charge of the production now, and it means a lot to me for a number of reasons. I'd like you to redo your designs, this time with as much lavish color as you can possibly summon. It should be a challenge to your imagination, Victoria, and I should think you'd welcome the opportunity to give full play to your fantasies, whatever they might be. As I recall, you once had a way of running from impossible dreams instead of finding ways to make them come true. Look upon this assignment as another chance, if you will. Dreams, I believe, have a way of catching up with their dreamers, no matter how far they may try to run."

She turned away, hating the knowing laughter that she saw in his brilliant eyes. He *was* speaking only of the costumes, or was he? She couldn't be sure. She knew only that his remarks were somehow insinuating, and his elusive reference to her past had unnerved her completely.

She pointed to her portfolio. "Just how much time do I have to complete this assignment?" she asked coldly.

"Well, I hate to rush you, but we're working against a tight deadline. I'd like you to be finished in a week—less than that, if possible."

She was fully struck by the staggering amount of unexpected work awaiting her. "That's absolutely unrealistic, and I'm sure you know it," she told him in a low, even voice while heated sparks lit her dark eyes.

"You should be able to handle it," he mused with a challenging little grin. "If not, you'll force me to call in someone from New York, and that would be a pity. I realize, of course, that things move more slowly here in Ann Arbor, although I was hoping that I could count on you. Be honest, if you don't feel up to it, my colleagues in New York will have no trouble with it at all."

The *gall* of the man. Vicky snatched up her portfolio as she regarded him through narrowed eyes. Yes, the years had changed Patrick Wallingford; his celebrated success and far-reaching reputation had swelled his ego insufferably. Well, if he thought she was just a small-town incompetent, he had quite another thought coming. She was a trained costume designer, and she was going to make sure he knew that beyond a shadow of doubt.

"You needn't worry about a thing. I'll have the new designs for you within the week," she snapped.

Having gotten his way, he only nodded smoothly, as though they were two strangers. "That will be splendid." He grinned. "Barnett told me that Mrs. Owens would do everything she could to assist me with the show. I'm delighted to see that he was right."

Vicky's flashing eyes met his fully as they stared at each other for a tense and bristling moment. Well, she certainly wasn't going to cower before this man just because he was a theatrical celebrity. She would meet him head-on, and she would win his respect, even if he gave it only with grudging approval.

"Patrick, darling! I've been looking for you everywhere, and I was beginning to think you'd disappeared on me forever. Whatever are you doing in here?"

Vicky turned to see a woman of striking beauty posing in a coquettish stance just inside the doorway. Luxuriant blond hair was piled dramatically on top of her head, and enormous, almond-shaped eyes dominated the flawless features of her face with a quality that was mesmerizing. She glided into the room as if she were making a stage entrance, the flowing folds of her loose-fitting emerald-green dress fluttering about her legs. It was Diana Galloway, and

Vicky looked on in fascination. She saw a woman about her own age with faint lines etched into a slight look of discontentment, her rosy mouth deliberately set in a fetching little pout.

Diana floated toward Patrick, carrying a five-pound box of gift-wrapped chocolates in her hands. "Have one, darling," she purred sweetly. "They're a present from that dear little man—Benson, I think his name is—and he's been just as darling and helpful as he can be."

Patrick's face suddenly glazed over with a carefully expressionless mask. "For heaven's sake, Diana, they're half gone," he muttered as he looked at the empty wrappers in the box. "You'll soon be getting fitted for your costumes, and you certainly want to avoid gaining weight." He ran his hand through his hair as he turned to Vicky. "This lady, by the way, is Victoria Owens. She'll be designing your costumes for the show."

Diana dipped her head in Vicky's direction, her Cupid's-bow mouth turning upward in a pretty smile. The greeting was courteous enough, yet there was a suggestion of cool regality in it, too—the star performer dealing with an underling.

"Ah, yes, of course. Well, I do hope you're nothing like my last designer in London. Francesca meant well, poor thing, but she was such a slowpoke. None of my costumes were ready until the dress rehearsal, and I practically went out of my mind with worry. Such a bother it was and so uncalled for." She paused, smiling graciously until she was satisfied that her little ancedote had made the proper impression on Vicky. Then, in a playful change of mood, she linked her arm lightly through Patrick's. "I know I've been a naughty girl, darling, eating all that candy, but you really mustn't scold me. I've been simply famished, and now that it's nearly six o'clock I must insist that you take me out to dinner. That dear old professor told me about a place in town that sounds charming—an old railroad station. If we sit by the windows, we can watch the trains go by."

She looked appealingly contrite and winsome, and Patrick smiled, in spite of the lines of fatigue that made him look drawn. "If you insist, Diana, and if it will make you stop gobbling up those god-awful chocolates, I think we can manage it. Where is this place?"

Diana covered her mouth coyly with her hand. "Oh, I forgot to ask."

Patrick looked at Vicky questioningly, one of his well-shaped eyebrows arching regally.

"I think the place you have in mind is the Gandy Dancer," Vicky replied with brisk courtesy, suddenly feeling like a social director. She gave the directions, her face carefully masking the resentment she felt within. When she finished, Patrick bid her a curt good-bye; Diana only nodded, then led him toward the door with bits of chatter and airy peals of laughter.

Vicky stared after them in silence. The next six weeks promised to mark a high point of thankless irritation in her life. Though the production had barely begun, she could scarcely wait until it was over and the visiting artists could go their merry way.

Chapter Three

The peal of carillon bells from the nearby tower rippled through the warm air in a joyous melody. Vicky, resting on the grassy campus lawn, allowed herself to luxuriate in a few stolen moments of relaxation. The past four days had allowed precious little time to herself since she had been so busy with redesigning the costumes. As a result, she had been cooped up indoors with her sketch pad for hours on end, calling feverishly upon her imagination to produce designs that would somehow meet the rigorous demands of Patrick Wallingford.

But for all her hard work, it had proven to be a rather heady flight upward, a challenging test of her most creative abilities. Her efforts had tapped imaginative powers she had never used before. As a result, she had left the restrictions of historical detail far behind and taken flight in rather lavish bursts of fancy. Well, if Patrick wanted more color, he would certainly find it with the new sketches, she mused. Fresh irritation washed over her as she recalled his blunt remarks once again. As a matter of fact, his words had sounded steadily in her ears throughout her long hours of concentration, goading her like a persistent alter ego to reach higher and higher. And she had done exactly that. He probably wouldn't react with speechless surprise when he saw her new designs—Patrick had apparently become far too cool and arrogant for that—but he could be expected to show some appreciation for her efforts. At least, she thought grimly, he'd better.

She plucked a dandelion from the grass before hugging her knees in her arms. Beside her lay a tall stack of books on costume design that she had just checked out of the library. She didn't want to overlook any source of research that might help in her uphill task. With their wealth of photographs and illustrations, these books were sure to fire her imagination more, so that her finished designs would be even more richly varied. Vicky sighed briefly, tickling her chin with the fuzzy yellow flower. She would continue to work at home later. For now she wanted nothing more than this deserved break with the bells singing so vibrantly in her ears.

A scattering of students were playing hooky as well, many stretched out nearby on blankets, clad in brief shorts and halter tops as they soaked up the bright sun. They were rushing the season, perhaps, for it was still early May. Nevertheless, the coming of spring was a cause for celebration in Michigan, and the memory of the harsh, frigid winter still lingered grimly in everyone's mind, making the arrival of warm weather that much sweeter.

"Isn't it far too fine a day for you to be saddled with all those dreary books?"

Vicky turned with a start at the unmistakable British inflection of the voice above her. With its resonant clarity it could belong only to Patrick. She looked up, her heart slamming in a perfectly adolescent reaction, and saw that she was right. He stood beside her with a rather bemused look of cordiality on his face, the sun catching his thick head of hair so that it glittered with gold and silver highlights. The theater was only yards away, and he must have just come from there for a leisurely walk across campus.

Then he was sinking down lightly to join her on the grass, the dashing lines of his lean frame covered by a pair of well-pressed khaki trousers and a green corduroy sports jacket that bore the distinct signs of having been impeccably hand tailored. Vicky had scarcely given a thought to her own appearance this afternoon, but at least her blue jeans showed off the long, slender lines of her legs to good advantage, and her kelly-green blouse, an old favorite of hers, looked presentable enough.

"I see that you've been doing your homework like a good girl," Patrick mused with a wry smile as he fingered one of her rather dusty books. "Such a pity on a beautiful day like this.

That instructor of yours must be quite a tyrant to assign you all this heavy reading." Then he closed the book playfully, his blue eyes fastening themselves on her with an engaging twinkle.

In spite of herself she burst into peals of laughter. "Yes, he's a real ogre," she said, her face wreathed in smiles. "But there doesn't seem to be any way that I can get around his fiendish demands, so I've decided to meet him head-on."

When he grinned, dimples seemed to flicker across his cheeks, appearing briefly and vanishing almost as soon as they had come. "A wise decision on your part," Patrick remarked with mock seriousness. "And perhaps you'll learn more than you bargained for. It's those old tyrants who usually make the very best of teachers."

A light breeze ruffled her black hair as the bells continued to chime merrily overhead. "Well, I hope you're right," she mused softly. "If I don't learn anything new and interesting from all this, then I'll certainly be disappointed." Suddenly she looked away from his laughing blue eyes and determinedly fixed her eyes on the tall white bell tower that loomed over the lawn with majestic dignity. Who would have thought it would be so delightfully easy to resume the playful banter she had once shared with this man years ago? But nothing was the same, and it was a little ridiculous of her to think it ever could be. The best way to handle this state of affairs was with a large measure of reserve.

"I confess you've roused all my tender sympathies," Patrick was saying lightly as he scooped up the largest pile of books in his arms. "You'll just have to let me help you carry these to wherever you're going." His eyes fell on the parked cars along Thayer Street. "Are you parked nearby?"

"I didn't drive, Patrick, I walked, and it's quite a way to my house." She picked up the rest of the books and stood with them in her arms, fully expecting him to hand her the ones he still held. "I'll have no trouble by myself. Anyway, I'm used to the walk."

"Then I'll join you, Victoria, if you don't mind," he said smoothly as he rose to his full height. "These are awfully heavy, and, being the ogre I am, you must let me bear my share of responsibility for them. Besides, I'd like a good walk. I haven't seen much of the town yet, and perhaps you can point out some points of interest along the way."

And so, as if by a small miracle, they were strolling side by side just as they had done years ago. This time, however, Ann Arbor provided the backdrop instead of stately, sophisticated London. How odd that things had been turned around in this way, Vicky thought as she stole a glance at his strong, well-chiseled profile. In London, of course, it had been Patrick who had shown her the sights, but now, apparently, it was her turn to do the same for him.

Beside her he was narrowing his eyes against the bright sun, taking in the activity on the Diag

with keen interest. He was as casually dressed
as anyone they passed, but as ever there was
that quality of difference about him. What was
it? Vicky wondered as she shyly turned away
from the warm little grin that he directed toward
her. Perhaps it was the vibrant sense of energy
that was ever present, tangible and pulsing
just beneath his surface. Whatever it was, Vicky
saw that other people noticed it, too, as he strode
briskly along. Who was this man? the calm university people with their rimless glasses and
backpacks seemed to wonder. And where had he
come from? It was obvious that he did not come
from here.

Soon they were walking along South University Street with its lively row of restaurants,
clothing stores, and book shops. As usual, there
was a throng of shoppers, many of them milling
under the bright awning at Logo's, where they
browsed through an eclectic assortment of books
displayed on the sidewalk. Ann Arbor was much
smaller than any town Patrick must have become accustomed to, but Vicky felt a small surge
of pride in it just the same. It had a bustling,
almost cosmopolitan quality that was rarely seen
in other small Midwestern cities.

"This is a refreshing change from the streets
of New York," Patrick chuckled as he studied
his companion with a look of fresh interest. "I
wasn't expecting to find everything that I have
here. It's been a pleasant surprise."

Whether he was referring to the town itself or

to something more personal, Vicky couldn't tell. Her heart raced as they turned onto Hill Street. Showing Patrick the landmarks of Ann Arbor's central campus had seemed, at first, safe activity, one that couldn't possibly stir up nostalgic memories. But they still lingered in the air, ghosts who refused to be safely banished.

Vicky knew she was overreacting, but she couldn't help herself. Quickly she scanned the rambling, Tudor-style fraternity houses on the street for something appropriate to say. She had passed these old dwellings hundreds of times, but they suddenly took on an alluring charm that she had never seen before. With their stucco and half-timbered trim they might be the setting for an Elizabethan drama in which she and this tall, vibrant Englishman had become the leading players. What an absurd idea. She was succumbing to the illusions of the theater again, and this time in the familiar surroundings of her own town.

"Ann Arbor is well known for its trees," she heard herself say in a carefully matter-of-fact tone. She fixed her glance overhead to a leafy canopy of giant oaks. "I believe that's how it came by its name in the first place."

She felt his eyes upon her. "That's interesting," he mused. "But tell me, Victoria, are your costume designs as good as your guided tour?"

She hugged her books to her with a twinkling smile. "You'll just have to wait to find out for yourself, won't you?"

The resonant sound of his laughter floated to her ears with a beguiling quality. "Then I look forward to it," he replied, but that brief statement, uttered so crisply, with a lilting hint of his Irish brogue, seemed to carry special meaning. Of course, Vicky reminded herself, this man had the power to make all words sound important, if he said something as simple as "Pass the butter," it was sure to leave his lips like a ringing line of poetry.

They approached the street where she lived, the comfortable old Victorian dwellings watching them from behind broad expanses of thick green lawns and shrubbery. It was very quiet here. Except for the occasional trill of a bird, there was not a sound to be heard.

"A lovely island of tranquillity in a world gone mad," mused Patrick slowly as he gazed at the weathervane on top of the gable of Professor Carmody's yellow house.

"Especially when you compare it with New York and London," Vicky replied with a quick little laugh, thinking that here, especially, Ann Arbor looked like any number of placid country towns. His eyes, however, were no longer fixed on the weathervane. They were seeking her own with that same sharp mixture of tenderness and intensity that she had never forgotten. Vicky couldn't turn away despite her best efforts. His eyes were much too blue, and they held her breathless with a riddle that was far too tantalizing. What exactly did he mean by "lovely island of tranquillity"? Did he mean Olivia Street, or could he possibly be referring to her instead?

"Well, we're here," she said faintly, stopping with flushed cheeks in front of her house. "This is where I live."

Her remark sounded lame and obvious to her ears, but Patrick, who was studying the sharply peaked roof and gingerbread trim of the old blue-and-white house, didn't seem to notice. "It suits you quite well, Victoria," he mused, his eyes gazing pensively at the house. "I take it you've lived here a long time."

"Yes, ever since I . . . well, yes," she answered, feeling flustered and not wishing to elaborate on past memories. The present moment was brimming with all the excitement she cared to handle.

Never in her wildest dreams had she imagined that Patrick Wallingford would be accompanying her under the lilac bushes along the path that led to her own front door. But he was, and his presence behind her was just as electric as she remembered. Should she ask him in? she wondered in a moment of panic. It would seem so strange to have this man enter the house where she and George had lived so peacefully.

But her question was answered for her. "Let me carry these books inside for you," she heard Patrick say with graceful courtesy. "I promise not to overstay my welcome. In fact, I have to meet with Diana on some family business. I'll be gone before you know it."

Those words, so casually spoken, seemed to

deflate a tiny balloon of hope that had begun to float in her mind. Their walk through town had been so sweet, a kind of innocent replay of how things used to be. Now, of course, the real world was intruding on this little trip through time in its cold, inevitable fashion. Diana was part of the reality, just as Bethanne, who by now must have returned from school, was.

As she opened the front door, Vicky realized Bethanne was home, but for once Bud was not monopolizing her time on the telephone. From the girl's upstairs bedroom came the dreamy refrain of her harp. She was actually practicing without having to be reminded, and Vicky smiled in surprise. This had turned out to be a strangely pleasant day, in more ways than one.

"First the chime of the bells and now this," Patrick murmured as he entered the high-ceilinged foyer with its yellow wallpaper. "Do my ears deceive me, or have I reached a kind of heaven on earth?"

Vicky laughed softly. "Not exactly. That's my daughter, Bethanne. She's actually quite a good harpist, but lately she's been far more interested in boys than in her music. I'm surprised to hear her practicing. Usually I have to prod her without mercy."

He nodded with understanding. "Ah, the terrible teens. My son, Christopher, is only twelve, but I fully expect he'll turn into something of an adolescent renegade. There's no escaping it, I'm told."

They smiled briefly at one another, two parents sharing the problems of raising their children. Vicky felt herself land on solid ground with a thud. The fact that Patrick was a father was not all that surprising, but his words brought her out of the past to remind her again of his marriage to Diana; the strumming of her daughter's harp was yet more proof of the major turns their lives had taken.

Patrick's gaze traveled to the top of the broad staircase from where the music wafted below like a serenade. "Your Bethanne is quite a talented girl. That kind of ability shouldn't go to waste." Patrick fastened his eyes on Vicky with an engaging smile. "Just tell me where I can put these books. I only hope they prove to be as weighty in information as they are in pounds."

She led him into the study with a shy burst of laughter. Since George's death she had adapted this room to her own needs. In the corner sat an easel, presently overflowing with her half-finished drawings for *Cyrano de Bergerac*. She had taped some of these designs to the bookshelves; others, those that she didn't like, lay in a rumpled pile on the floor. The room looked wildly messy, but it still bore signs of George's studious presence. He had spent long hours in this room working on research and class notes, and the shelves were lined with his impressive collection of books about Shakespeare. Under the window was George's antique rolltop desk with his favorite family photographs displayed on it in a cluster.

Vicky felt a tremor of uneasiness. This was still very much her husband's room, and Patrick's appearance in it almost seemed an intrusion.

He was surveying the personal mementos about him with a look of warm curiosity. "Such a cozy place to live and work in," he murmured softly. She thought she heard that wistful note of sadness in his voice once again, although she couldn't be sure. "Ah, I can see you've been working hard," he said, immediately resuming his jaunty air of cordiality. He walked with interest to the costume designs, which were hanging in front of him, studying them closely. "Yes, these are much better. You catch on quickly, in spite of the resistance you put up the other day."

She placed her pile of books on the desk with a wry grin. "Well, I'm always open to new ideas. Living in Ann Arbor hasn't put me as far behind the times as you seem to think."

He smiled with his eyes as he finally unloaded his heavy pile of books next to her stack. "Living here has done you good, Victoria. I'm glad." He glanced at his wristwatch in a suddenly restrained manner. "Ah, but I really must be going now. It's nearly five, and I suppose you'll have to fix dinner for your husband."

Now was Vicky's chance to tell Patrick that the evening meal she would prepare would be only for her and Bethanne. George's scholarly presence still lingered in this room, but he was gone, and Patrick had to be told. She watched him with slightly parted lips, urging herself to speak. But she remained silent once again, maddeningly unable to leave the protective domain of her foolish hiding place.

Patrick's eyes were scanning the photographs on George's desk, which included pictures of Vicky and Bethanne, as well as snapshots from various family vacations. When his eyes fell on an informal portrait of George, Vicky reacted with a crimson flush of embarrassment. It had been taken at a university function and later presented to her by the faculty after George's death. George had been in an especially relaxed mood when the photo was taken, his eyes twinkling with humor from behind his glasses. But underneath this pleasant image was his name in gold letters, accompanied by a brief but unmistakable message: "In memorium, 1927–1982."

Patrick was examining the portrait, a perplexed frown creasing his forehead. "I'm sorry," he murmured softly. Then his blue eyes searched her face anew. "Still, you might have told me, you know."

Her face felt as if it were on fire. "Well, I . . . I was going to. I don't know why I didn't sooner, but . . ." Vicky's voice trailed off as she looked away. She could offer no rational excuse for not mentioning her widowhood, and she wondered if Patrick would be angry or would make a cryptic and biting remark.

"You were hiding again, Victoria," he murmured in a gentle, husky voice. "First behind a veil and now behind a memory." A tender smile was beginning to play about the corners of his lips, and he peered again at the portrait as if he were trying to solve a riddle. "Such a kind face," he mused softly. "But I think you're doing him an injustice. For years he was husband, father, and provider. Surely now it is time to let the poor man rest in peace."

Patrick carefully and deliberately placed the picture facedown on the desk. In doing so, he removed a barrier between them, and they gazed at each other with the same, sweet expectancy they had shared in London. His face drew nearer, and before she closed her eyes Vicky was wondrously aware again of the vitality of his presence and of the sweet, faintly musky scent that emanated from him.

She met his lips with a small, tremulous rush of emotion. Had eighteen years really passed? His mouth explored her own, and the kiss filled her with a warmth that flooded her veins. Everything else might have changed with time, but this was just the same. When she felt him wrap his arms about her, gathering her to his strong, graceful body, she could only respond in kind, filled with a need that grew more heated as he pulled her closer. Her bones felt like flowing liquid, and she seemed to melt against him, her breasts tight against his broad chest, her hips pressed hard against his. The rest of the world fell away, and there was only this moment of incredible sweetness.

Patrick slowly drew back, his eyes searching

her face with a hundred unspoken questions as she gazed up at him in silence. Was it really possible to step back in time as if the present did not exist? What could this moment mean? It could only lead to yet another dead end for her and Patrick, couldn't it?

Vicky was barely aware of running footsteps on the stairway. When a voice from behind her called out cheerfully, "Hey, Mom, what did you think of that?" she turned around with a sudden start.

Bethanne stood barefoot in the doorway, the broad smile on her mouth quickly changing to a round O of surprise. "Oops, I didn't know there was anyone . . . I mean, I'm sorry if I—" She popped her hand over her lips, wide eyes fixed on the handsome stranger standing so close to her mother.

Dear God, how was one supposed to handle a situation like this? Vicky wondered in a fit of awkward panic. But Patrick simply smiled at the girl, his poise fully intact.

"This isn't quite so startling as it may seem, Bethanne," he said with an air of quiet confidence. "You see, your mother and I knew each other a long time ago in London. Memories for people our age hold a special kind of magic."

Bethanne nodded, but her face still held a look of astonishment. A tense silence followed before Vicky was able to collect herself, drawing a long breath before she made the introductions.

"Now that I've become acquainted with your

music, I'm most happy to meet you in person," Patrick said as he warmly shook Bethanne's limp hand. "You play quite beautifully, you know."

A blush rose to the girl's cheeks at this flattering compliment from a man who seemed as courtly as he was handsome. He was different from the other men who normally crossed her schoolgirl path, and she was able to respond with only a few stammered phrases. Nevertheless, Vicky saw that this unexpected visitor was making quite an impression on her normally intrepid child. Patrick was apparently able to charm all women, no matter what their age.

"I suppose daily practice requires a good deal of discipline and sacrifice of your leisure time," Patrick was saying in a sympathetic voice. "I'm not a musician myself, but a good friend of mine teaches at the London College of Music and has acquainted me with some of the intricacies of the harp. I know it's not an easy instrument to play, and I take my hat off to you."

Bethanne was staring at him in awe. "Oh, I'd practice every minute if I could study at a place like that. That's where I've always wanted to go, but Mom says we can't afford it. Of course, we're not poor, but the tuition . . ."

"There are schools of·music around here, Bethanne. You know that," Vicky put in firmly, not wanting to discuss the family finances in front of Patrick.

"I know, but Michigan is so boring." Her daughter sighed and then her face colored with embarrassment as she turned to Patrick. "I hope you don't think I sound like a spoiled brat. I guess a person can learn anywhere if they really want to, even in Michigan. It's not so bad, really. I've been taking lessons for years, and everyone keeps telling me that all that effort shouldn't go to waste. Especially Mom."

"Well, your mother is quite right," Patrick answered lightly. "If you keep it up, you could have a fine career in store for you. Have you had a chance to do any solo performing in front of an audience, Bethanne?"

"Well, some," the girl admitted with shy pride. "At music camp last summer I played Respighi's 'Siciliana.' "

He dipped his head in recognition of the difficult piece. "That's quite an accomplishment. I asked because I am thinking of adding some music to the production that your mother and I are working on. It seems we'll be dealing with some rather complicated set changes, and during the interim the audience might appreciate the talents of a good harpist. At any rate, your music would be fitting for the mood of the play."

Bethanne took this in with a stunned look of amazement. "Oh, but I . . . I mean, I've never really done anything like *that* before. Do you think I really could?"

"I think you could," Patrick assured her in a voice of brisk confidence. "Of course, the play hasn't been entirely cast, and it's still in the planning stages. Nevertheless, I'd like you to keep it in mind. You will, won't you, while you continue practicing?"

The girl nodded in speechless wonder while Vicky continued to watch this interaction in much the same way. Patrick Wallingford had dazzled two women in the same household in a matter of minutes, as though he were the Pied Piper. His effect on Bethanne seemed too good to be believed, and yet if it encouraged her in her music, what harm could it possibly do?

Patrick, with another hasty glance at his wristwatch, seemed intent upon keeping his appointment. He said good-bye to Bethanne, and Vicky had no choice but to show him to the front porch.

"Patrick, are you really serious about keeping all those promises?"

"Which promises do you mean?"

The dancing lights in those azure eyes confused her. She had been referring to Bethanne's opportunity to perform, but as she gazed up at him Vicky was aware of the kiss they had shared only moments ago. That, too, had been a kind of promise. Or was she deluding herself?

He tweaked her nose playfully. "I'm a most serious man, Victoria. You ought to know that I never make promises I cannot keep." Then he chuckled. "As a matter of fact, I promised Diana that I'd meet her in half an hour, and that's a promise not to be broken at any cost. The lady doesn't like to be kept waiting, as I'm sure you'll find out soon enough."

He ran lightly down the steps of the old gingerbread porch and past the arbor of lilacs to the sidewalk. Vicky sighed as she watched him disappear from sight. Then she returned to the house; Bethanne stood waiting in the foyer, still starry-eyed with wonder.

"Oh, Mom, is he . . . is he the one you were telling me about the other day? That actor you met in London?"

Vicky looked carefully into her daughter's face to see the same vulnerability she felt herself. Nevertheless, she was the parent, and it was up to her to set a realistic example. "Yes, Bethanne, but it's nothing to get so excited about, not really."

"It is, too," Bethanne protested with a delighted giggle. "He's really a hunk, especially for a guy his age. Besides, I don't mind. Now that you've got a boyfriend of your own, maybe you won't be so hard on me and Bud."

"He is not my boyfriend, Bethanne, so don't jump to any wild conclusions. He . . . well, we haven't seen each other for a long time, and—" She stopped in mid-sentence, unable to finish the thought in a rational way.

Bethanne eyed her with a knowing twinkle. "Mom, you look so cute when you blush."

"All right, Miss Teenage America, not another word from you," Vicky replied with firm good humor as she placed her arm around the girl's shoulder and began leading her to the kitchen. "It's time to fix dinner, and I'm enlisting your help with the mashed potatoes. You just settle down, or I'm afraid that imagination will carry you right off the face of this earth."

Though her words of advice were directed at her fifteen-year-old daughter, Vicky knew that, for her own good, she had better heed them herself.

Chapter Four

❦

"Almost finished," Vicky murmured as she cinched her yellow tape measure around David Lang's waist. He had, it turned out, been chosen for the role of Cyrano de Bergerac, after all. Her assistants were similarly engaged nearby with other actors. Now that the play was cast, the costume room had become a beehive of activity and would remain that way until the production ended.

Today there was an extra undercurrent of excitement in the air. The entire cast and crew were to be honored that evening at a reception given by Dr. Samuel Chamberlain, the president of the university. Vicky had never been inside Dr. Chamberlain's stately mansion, and she knew that his hospitality was a special gesture of welcome for Patrick and Diana. Even so, it was unprecedented for the rest of them to be asked as well.

A young actor suddenly appeared in the doorway, and Vicky looked up questioningly. The cast was so large that, at this early stage, it was hard to know everyone by name. As the young man, a handsome blond with a flamboyant, theatrical air, began to speak, Vicky was able to identify him as Michael Rowland, who had been cast as Christian de Neuvillette.

"At least it's cooler down here," he exclaimed as he began to fan himself dramatically. "You just missed fireworks upstairs that were absolutely unbelievable." Then he positioned himself against a table, obviously full of some juicy tidbit of gossip and wanting to arouse everyone's curiosity.

"Now that you've dangled the bait so temptingly, I guess I'll just have to go for it," spoke up Nancy Foster wryly. "What gives?"

"Well, far be it from poor, humble me to criticize my betters," Michael replied with a flourish. "But it looks like our two distinguished artists have just gone up in flames. They had a regular brouhaha onstage about the blocking for the bakery scene. Galloway insisted she was being upstaged, and Wallingford insisted she wasn't. She grew very huffy when he absolutely refused to change a thing and finally—get this—she threw the script right in his face. Most of the cast and half the faculty were watching. I would have thought those two would want a little more privacy for their famous tempers, but I guess they like playing to a full house."

Michael was enjoying the attention he had gained at being the bearer of such news, and Vicky regarded him with silent disapproval. The theater was often a hotbed of rumor and gossip, and although she disliked the young man's sensational way of reporting it, she had no choice but to hear him. Besides, as much as she hated to admit it, she was as interested as the others to hear what had happened. Perhaps even more so, she conceded ruefully.

"And that, I fear, was only the beginning," Michael continued with relish. "At that point Wallingford informed the lady in no uncertain terms that if she was unable to behave like a rational adult, she should leave the theater. Unfortunately she took him up on his suggestion and stormed out like a flash of lightning. You could almost hear the electricity sizzle between them."

"But that's awful," breathed Nancy Foster, her tape measure dangling idly. "She can't just walk out in the middle of a rehearsal like that. Besides, she's a professional actress. Isn't she supposed to be serving as a role model for the rest of the cast?" Her bewildered young face turned questioningly to Vicky. "What do you think, Mrs. Owens? I mean, you've been around the theater for a long time. Isn't this a bit unusual?"

Vicky sighed as she placed her notebook with the actor's measurements beside her sewing machine. "Well, I can't really comment about it because I didn't see it," she explained carefully. "But I do know life in the theater is full of surprises. Let's not jump to conclusions, though. I'm sure that Mr. Wallingford and Miss Galloway will be able to settle their . . . differences. They're both professionals, after all, and they haven't earned respect in their field for nothing."

She had hoped that her words would have a calming effect and would serve to dampen any potential rumors that might spread. Working in the theater was always a team effort, and if the team members grew suspicious of one another, the production could only suffer as a result. Nevertheless, Michael Rowland, still enamored of his spicy gossip, seemed unwilling to simmer down.

"Oh, yes, they've had years of experience in mutual warfare," he said with youthful cynicism. "From what I hear, they can't live with each other, but they can't live without each other, either. So it seems we are about to have one of the more tempestuous love sagas of the modern stage played out before our very eyes."

His remarks were met by giggles before Vicky finally stepped in to change the subject. "It's high time for you to be measured, especially since you have a party to attend in a little while," she told Michael as she unrolled her tape measure. He then stood almost docilely before her, arms outstretched and sharp tongue silenced, at least for the moment.

Shortly thereafter, Michael and the others fled from the room like a band of impatient gypsies to get ready for the party. Vicky, however, stayed behind for a few minutes, arranging bolts of fabric and trim, which the students had left in disarray. She couldn't help but wonder if the two visiting celebrities would be in the mood to function as guests of honor during the evening festivities. Still, no matter how bad their stormy reunion might be, they would certainly be obliged to show up, if only for the sake of appearances. If nothing else, she concluded wryly, it should prove to be an interesting evening.

But Vicky was determined to enjoy herself. Patrick's attentions to her the other day had obviously been just a nostalgic little game, and it would be absurd for her to take them seriously. Yes, they had shared some sweet moments, but all that lay behind them. If Patrick looked to the past occasionally, it was only because his present, at least for the time being, had taken a difficult turn.

At last she removed the dark smock that had virtually become her uniform. The silken fabric of the teal-blue dress hugged her slender figure. She slipped on the pair of high-heeled, thin-strapped sandals that she had brought from home, and her outfit was complete. A glance in the full-length mirror told her that she looked quite nice. The dress, a new and unusually costly one for her modest budget, had been worth every penny, and she smoothed it around her hips with satisfaction. Its very simplicity gave it an air of quiet elegance that would be appropriate for the party, and the jewellike tone of blue was the perfect foil for her dark hair and eyes. For a moment she wondered what Diana Galloway would be wearing, but she pushed the thought from her mind. Diana, no matter what she might wear, would command attention tonight as an important guest of honor along with Patrick Wallingford. Vicky Owens, on the other hand, could only expect to sit pleasantly on the sidelines in cordial tribute to this celebrated pair. It would be an awkward role for her to play, perhaps, but she had to do it, if only for the sake of appearances.

"It's getting late, Cinderella. I hope you're not waiting down here for an invitation from your fairy godmother."

Patrick's image suddenly appeared in the mirror. A lightweight gray suit covered his tall frame with an air of casual elegance, and a lock of thick hair fell onto his forehead. There were lines of weariness about his mouth, but they softened perceptibly as he watched her reflection in the mirror.

Vicky smiled without turning around. "Oh, but my fairy godmother has already stopped by. In fact, I was just about to leave with her blessing. I don't have much time, you see, because at midnight she'll change me back into a pumpkin."

Patrick's dimples appeared on his face in response to her words. They had amused each other in London with such whimsical exchanges, and now, as if no time had passed at all, they were sharing them again. "Well, then, you must let me help you make the best of the time you do have," he replied with a little bow. "May I escort you to the ball, milady?"

Their images in the glass told Vicky that in appearance they were well matched; two tall, slender people whose different coloring contrasted pleasantly. But the mirror, like the stage, often provided no more than a fetching illusion. She turned suddenly to face him. "Don't you think that might pose something of a problem? What about Diana?"

His blue eyes held her dark ones firmly. "As you've doubtlessly heard, Diana has gone off in one of her huffs. I hadn't planned to escort her tonight, anyway. I'm asking you."

"I see," Vicky replied slowly as a disturbing thought began to flicker in her mind. "But that would put me in an awkward position. I really have no desire to become the third party in an emotional triangle."

Patrick's low laugh was filled with a note of delighted incredulity. "Whatever can you mean, Victoria? Diana is my ex-wife, just as George Owens is your late husband. Those are past bonds that have little to do with our present. You and I are free to go out with whomever we choose."

"Well, that may be true enough," Vicky conceded. "Still, you have to admit that for an ex-wife, Diana seems to play a prominent role in your life."

"Only as an actress, Victoria, one who needs firm direction at this point in her muddled life." He sighed briefly as he searched her face. "There's really nothing else left between us anymore. If you expect her to make a heated scene, I can promise you she won't. She's in capable hands with Benson Barnett, who was last seen calling her a cab and doing everything he could to soothe her ruffled feathers. The man promised me that as my assistant he'd take on these problems when they arose, and I can see that he means to keep his word. Diana will calm down eventually—she always does."

What he said sounded logical enough, but even as an actress, Diana's lingering presence still seemed too close for comfort. "Yes, but . . ."

"But nothing." He smiled warmly as he took her hand lightly and persuasively in his. "You must come with me. Besides, I don't know where the party is being held. I'm a visitor in town. Surely it won't be out of place for a cordial faculty member to help me find my way."

In spite of herself, she smiled happily. Patrick had made his point with his customary charm, and under the circumstances it seemed foolish for Vicky to refuse. If others observed them together, what of it? Patrick Wallingford was the play's director, and she was the costume designer. That there might be more to their joint appearance was something that the public didn't have to know about. She would certainly do her part to act with discretion, and she felt sure that Patrick, too, would do the same.

Their walk to the party through the gathering dusk was a brief one; the president's house was only minutes from the main campus. The mansion was fully lit, and as they proceeded along the front walk Vicky felt a fresh tremor of excitement. Invitations to visit Dr. Chamberlain were rarely issued to junior faculty members such as herself. Of course, it was only because of Patrick that she was here, and in his presence her town took on an undeniable glamour it had never seemed to offer before.

They were met by Dr. Chamberlain, who greeted them at the front door unpretentiously. "Ah, Mr. Wallingford," he said, shaking Patrick's hand warmly. "I'm honored to meet you at last and to personally welcome you to our university." His distinguished face, with his shock of pure white hair and silver-rimmed glasses, was familiar to Vicky through newspaper photographs, but she had never met him in person. "And this lovely lady, I presume, is the talented Miss Galloway."

Patrick's hand on her elbow felt firm and secure as he guided her into the foyer. "This is Victoria Owens, the talented costume designer of your own theater department," he explained with a charming smile.

Dr. Chamberlain bowed graciously as he shook her hand. "Of course," he murmured. "I only regret that our faculty is such a large one that I don't always have the chance to know individual members as well as I should. I'm certainly delighted to meet you." Then he ushered them through the elegant foyer into a sweeping dining room with an Oriental rug. The arched windows were framed by sashed velvet draperies in a deep, luxurious shade of blue. The cast and crew of *Cyrano de Bergerac* were gathered, all of them on their best behavior as they sedately helped themselves to the feast spread on the mahogany table. Bubbling quiches stood on platformed silver trays, sending a tempting aroma of cheese and spices through the air. There was also an intriguing assortment of appetizers: jumbo stuffed mushrooms, spicy sausages, and dainty meatballs wrapped in puff pastry.

Dr. Chamberlain handed Vicky and Patrick two white china plates with a courteous bow. "Please help yourselves," he told them. "And join me on the terrace when you've finished. There'll be entertainment out there shortly, and I had hoped that we might be able to enjoy it together."

Vicky nodded mutely, too awestruck for the moment to say a word. With Patrick at her side she was being treated by Samuel Chamberlain as if she were a royal dignitary. It was a heady feeling, one she had never experienced. Patrick seemed comfortable enough, however, and apparently was used to such treatment. He responded with his usual charm, causing Dr. Chamberlain's solemn face to break into a broad, spontaneous smile.

When their plates were heaped with tempting appetizers and an array of colorful little petits fours, they made their way through the chatter-

ing crowd to the open French doors leading to
the terrace. Outside, the night air was warm
and fragrant, and hanging lanterns provided a
gentle source of illumination against the black
velvet sky. Garden tables and chairs had been
arranged in a cozy fashion, many of them already occupied. As Vicky looked about, she saw
with some relief that Diana was not among the
crowd. Was it possible that, after her tempera-
mental outburst, she wouldn't appear at all?

But Patrick was able to handle her absence with
a well-rehearsed gallantry. "Miss Galloway was
a little under the weather tonight," he explained in response to Dr. Chamberlain's tactfully phrased question. "Unfortunately she suf-
fers from migraine headaches on occasion, and
this seems to be one of those times. She was
very sorry not to be able to come, but it just
wasn't possible. She sends her sincere regrets."

If he was embarrassed or angered by her conspicuous absence, only the slightly drawn expression on his face revealed it. Vicky couldn't
help but admire the courtesy with which he had
covered up the reasons for her behavior. Still,
she sensed that it wasn't easy for him to have to
make her excuses, especially after the way she
had treated him. There was no reason for a
professional actress to challenge the authority
of her director so rudely, especially in front of
students.

Vicky stole a glance at Patrick as he chatted
quietly with Dr. Chamberlain, the flickering

candlelight from the table softening the lines of fatigue around his intense blue eyes. For the first time in her life she felt a flicker of sympathy for him. Under that demeanor of worldly success and impeccable polish, there seemed to be a vulnerable human being. She suddenly realized that he must have been hurt many times by the abrasive antics of his beautiful ex-wife, perhaps deeply hurt.

The evening passed pleasantly. Patrick and Dr. Chamberlain chatted congenially about the theater, often including Vicky in the conversation. Of course, it wasn't as if she had nothing to say; it was just that, until now, she had never had the chance to say it in such distinguished company. After a while she was able to relax, aided considerably by Patrick's amusing anecdotes and the graceful aplomb with which he handled himself. Soon enough the three of them sat laughing together in an easy way. Why, this was more fun than she'd had in a long time.

A group of pantomimists, students from the theater department, appeared in white face and dramatic black-and-white costumes, and they were met by a burst of applause from everyone on the terrace. Looking like a group of animated dominoes, they began their performance by stationing themselves directly in front of Patrick, who was plainly delighted by their humorous skits. A round of champagne followed, accompanied by the tricks of several jugglers, who easily wound their way between the tables, dazzling the guests with their flying balls and amusing them with quaint jokes and riddles.

Vicky's face glowed softly with enjoyment as she turned to Patrick. He could never be called a relaxed man; his ever-present intensity and driving energy were far too prominent for that. But now, at least, he seemed content. The lines of fatigue had all but disappeared from the corners of his mouth, and Vicky was glad to see that his earlier confrontation with Diana seemed to be forgotten.

The guests began to leave a short time later, the light dresses of the girls and women fluttering softly behind them like the wings of butterflies. Dr. Chamberlain escorted Vicky and Patrick to the door to see them off, his solemn eyes full of respect and his handshake warm and sincere. He turned to Vicky after he had said good-bye to Patrick. "It's been a pleasure, Mrs. Owens. It's gratifying to know that our theater department has capable people to work with visitors such as Patrick. Please don't wait for an invitation next time. My door is always open to the faculty, and I'd be most happy to see you again."

Outside, the street was quiet and fragrant, softly lit by a vast array of twinkling stars in the night sky. Vicky sighed peacefully.

"Did you have a good time?" Patrick asked as he guided her across South University Street. The firm touch of his arm sent spears of warmth through her body.

She laughed softly as they approached the ornate Gothic turrets of the law school building, its windows twinkling with yellow lights. "Oh, yes," she breathed. "I almost felt like visiting royalty."

"Well, perhaps you might be, after all," he murmured. "Look, you have a castle right here that you can use as your very own stage set."

She laughed aloud in protest. "The only problem is that it's not a castle, at all. It's only the U of M law school building."

"But you're wrong, Victoria. Tonight it *is* a castle, if you want it to be, and those faces in the windows don't belong to students burning the midnight oil but to fair ladies and knights in search of a long-lost princess. Who knows? It could be you. You'll never find out if you refuse to try."

She smiled ruefully, enjoying his playfulness, but unwilling to participate in it herself. It was dangerous to allow your dreams to rule your life, wasn't it? Besides, what if you were only blinding yourself with impossible illusions? How crushingly disappointed you would be when reality intruded, and how ridiculous you would appear to the rest of the world. It was easy enough for Patrick to play these little games with her, but it was her life, and in just six short weeks he would be gone from it.

Nevertheless, the walk home continued to be pleasant, and once again Vicky was filled with wonder that he was really here. But he was, and his presence was more real to her than all the other sights along the way.

"Would you like a cup of coffee?" she asked shyly when they had reached her front door. "I mean, if it isn't too late . . ."

"It's not too late for me," he assured her with a dimpled smile. He followed her into the cozy living room, with its comfortable country furniture and its long white lace curtains that billowed in the gentle breeze.

"Such a lovely room," Patrick murmured softly as he looked about him. "My grandmother in Ireland had curtains like these."

"Well, I suppose they are rather old-fashioned," she admitted, "but I guess that's why I like them." His eyes met hers with a bittersweet poignancy that caught her by surprise. "Well, maybe I should make the coffee now."

"Wait, Victoria. Please. You ran away from me once, but I don't see why it has to happen again. Not unless you want it to." His hands, long-fingered and lean, began to cradle her face, tipping her chin up so that she had no choice but to gaze into his penetrating blue eyes. "Do you?"

Vicky shook her head silently. At this moment it was the only answer she could possibly give him. Then he was embracing her almost possessively, his arms enfolding her so tightly that she could feel the beat of his heart against her own. His mouth claimed hers with warm insistence, tender at first, but with a hunger that grew deeper, more demanding as he continued. He parted her lips with his probing tongue in such a sweet invasion of her private self that she met it with a little moan. Oh, it had been too long since she had known such pleasure, and her body cried out for more as desire flooded her veins like slow, thick honey. When his tongue began to speak to her with a silent, rhythmic intimacy, she could only answer him in kind, revealing her longing in a way that no words could ever express. And when she heard him groan deep within his throat, she knew that her message was clear.

"How I love the taste of you, Victoria. You're just as sweet as always," she heard him murmur huskily into her ear. "Oh, God, why did you leave me? It hurt so much."

His face bore a look of anguish that went straight to her heart. "I don't know, Patrick," she whispered in a soft rush, but even as the words left her lips Vicky remembered that eighteen years ago his intensity had somehow frightened her. It had seemed to demand more than she dared to give. "But that was all so long ago," she said softly. "This is now."

With eyes closed she felt his hands move toward her breasts, exploring the soft swell under the thin fabric of her dress. His fingers were both firm and delicate, and her body, so long untouched, responded in a heated rush that made her senses spin. They eased themselves down to the sofa and the length of his body pressed upon her own.

Vicky heard him murmur her name, his voice falling like a breathless melody in her ear. Then his lips were crushing hers in an openmouthed kiss of such depth that she knew only a wild surge of joy. The rest of the world faded into welcome oblivion.

But the world, it seemed, had an uncanny way of intruding. Vicky became faintly aware of voices outside, dim at first, but growing louder and more exuberant as they reached the front door.

"Bud, that's got to be the craziest thing you ever said," she heard Bethanne exclaim in a peal of giddy laughter. Then she lowered her voice dramatically. "Shush, will you? My mom's probably getting ready for bed if she's not asleep already."

Vicky sat bolt upright like a jack-in-the-box, forcing Patrick to take the same position by the sheer energy of her movements. With one hand she frantically began to button her dress, and with the other she lunged for the small TV set on the table and flicked it on.

"It's Bethanne and her boyfriend," she explained through clenched teeth as Patrick watched her with a startled expression. "They'll be in any minute."

"Oh, good God, why now of all times?" he said almost fiercely, his eyes still blazing with blue fire.

"You may have forgotten, but Bethanne happens to live here, too."

He sighed, settling the lines of his lean body into a posture of resignation. Then he turned toward the TV; Sonny Applebee, the local weatherman, was laughing loudly in response to one of his well-worn jokes.

"This is my favorite way to end an evening," Patrick drawled in dry amusement as he lightly sought her hand. "I always say there's nothing like getting a good weather report before turning in for the night."

"Just watch the program, will you?" she pleaded with a laugh as she turned her attention back to Sonny Applebee.

When Bethanne dashed into the room, breathless as usual, Patrick and Vicky were seated on the sofa, two staid adults who seemingly had nothing better to do than watch TV for entertainment.

Chapter Five

In the hectic days that followed, Vicky saw Patrick often, but they were never alone. They simply had no chance for that. At the theater they invariably found themselves in the middle of the cast and crew, who always needed their attention about something. When Patrick came to call at Olivia Street, Bethanne was usually there, her time at home increasing because of Bud's new hours as a bellboy at a local hotel.

Of course, things could have been worse. Patrick was an excellent influence on Bethanne, and in his presence she was taking her music more seriously than she had in months. She often played for him, listening in rapt silence to his words of encouragement when she had finished.

Vicky couldn't help but be glad for this positive turn in her daughter's life, but even so she found herself growing slightly impatient. In Bethanne's presence she and Patrick could only be as two jolly old friends; whatever deeper feelings they might have for each other had to be guarded carefully. If this was the second beginning of some sort of romantic involvement, it was getting off to a rather confused and public start, Vicky concluded. But maybe that was the way things had to be. Family and job responsibilities couldn't be ignored, and romance, it seemed, had to be crammed in whenever time allowed, if it managed to fit in, at all.

Still, she was glad for any chance she had to be with him, even if she did have to share him with other people. Patrick was, unequivocally, the best director she had ever worked with. His ability to inspire the student actors into giving their best performances was uncanny. In a few short weeks he had them unabashedly hanging on his every word, not because he was overbearing—he never had to resort to those kinds of tactics—but because his expert control and brilliant theatrical vision had won their respect.

Even Diana Galloway seemed to settle down as best she could under his brisk authority. She still remained sensitive to the criticism he occasionally had to give her, but during these tense moments Benson Barnett obligingly stepped in to smooth things over. It was a good thing, too. Diana seemed to have no end of problems in playing her role, but Benson, with unfailing diplomacy and patience, calmed Diana down when others seemed ready to tear their hair out.

"I suppose I can be something of a handful, but how can I help it when my poor brain seems to be turning to fudge?" Diana admitted to Vicky one evening after a grueling rehearsal. Diana compulsively nibbled away on a large candy bar. "Of course, I know there are some people who think I'm too old to play Roxane. Not that I should listen to them—they're nothing but a bunch of jealous cats. It's just so terribly hard for an artist to concentrate with all that nasty backbiting." She sighed heavily as she posed before the mirror, her face as beautiful as ever but showing the unmistakable signs of her thirty-eight years. "What do you think, darling? Is there still some life left in me?"

Until now Diana had seemed only casually aware of her costumer, and Vicky was surprised at this burst of confidence. As she watched the actress's reflection in the mirror, however, she had a sudden flash of understanding. Like many performers, Diana had relied heavily on her beautiful face, but now that her youth was passing she evidently faced a challenge she wasn't sure she could handle.

"We're about the same age, Diana," Vicky said with a smile. "As far as I'm concerned, there's a lot of life left in *both* of us."

Diana moaned as she briefly shut her eyes. "I don't even like to think about it. The idea of growing old gracefully is absolutely appalling. I'm sure I'll never manage it."

"It's really not all that bad," Vicky offered softly.

Diana studied her companion, unassuming and sensibly clad in her dark blue smock. "Not for you, maybe. Sometimes I think that life begins at our age for people who have never known the limelight, but it ends there for those of us who have."

"Oh, I don't think that's true at all," Vicky said with a rush of sympathy. It was odd for her to be comforting this woman, perhaps, but Diana seemed to need words of encouragement. "Life ends only when you're ready to give it up, and you're a long way from that, Diana. For one thing, you have a lead part in the play, so you certainly don't want to let your audience down." She paused, searching for a message of extra kindness. "Besides, you look lovely in your costumes. I'm sure no one half your age could look as good."

Her words seemed to do the trick. Diana smiled with some satisfaction as she gazed into the mirror, smoothing her thick, luxurious hair with the palm of her hand. "I hope you're right," she said as she examined her face with the utmost care. Then she popped her hand over her mouth in a little gasp of surprise. "Oh, I almost forgot. Patrick wanted to see how that satin gown will look under the lights, and he's been waiting for me all this time." Her long-lashed blue eyes fell imploringly on Vicky. "You simply must help me put it on. Patrick can be so difficult when I keep him waiting. He just doesn't understand that I can't live my life by a clock. If I'm not onstage soon, he'll probably explode again."

After a whirl of activity Diana stood breathlessly in the gown while Vicky labored to zip up the back. The trouble was, it no longer fit. Since Vicky had taken Diana's measurements, the actress had gained about ten pounds, obviously the result of her sweet tooth.

"Oh, *no*," Diana wailed. "Patrick will be simply furious. What am I going to do? I can't run out onstage with the dress open in the back. Everyone will know how fat I've gotten, and it'll be so embarrassing. I'll just *die*." Miserably, she wriggled her arms out of the billowing sleeves and let the shiny creation fall in a dispirited heap on the floor. "Tell Patrick I had to leave, will you? I know it's awful, but I simply can't face him now."

Minutes later she vanished in a fretful flurry, refusing to listen to Vicky's attempts to calm her down. Why, she was every bit as immature as Bethanne, in spite of her age and her years in professional theater. Had she always been this way? Vicky wondered. Or were these childish outbursts the result of an inability to accept her age? Whatever the reason, she was undeniably the most scatterbrained, trying woman to work with.

"Do you know what happened to Diana? The lighting man and I have been waiting for her to show up onstage in her costume." In the doorway Patrick appeared harried and distracted, his mouth pressed into a humorless line that was quite unlike his usual self.

"She . . . she just left, I'm afraid," Vicky replied softly. "I tried to convince her to stay, but there was no stopping her. The costume was a little tight, and she . . . well, she thought you'd be upset with her."

"Good Lord, she's just kept the whole crew waiting up there, and all she can think about is herself." He brushed a strand of his hair from his forehead in a distracted gesture. "Where's the costume? I hope to God she hasn't seen fit to destroy the evidence of her latest binge."

Vicky lifted the dress off the rack. "It's right here. Maybe you could have someone walk across the stage with it. I mean, if all you want to do is see how it looks under the lights—"

"No, that won't do," he snapped, making her feel as if this unpleasant situation were her fault. "It can't be dragged along—there has to be a body inside. How about you, Vicky? You seem to be the only woman left in the building."

"But I—"

"Please don't give me an argument. Just put the thing on and be out there in five minutes. I've spent twelve full hours in this building today, and I'd like to leave sometime before midnight." Then he turned and disappeared as abruptly as he had arrived.

Vicky felt a surge of indignation. It was awkward enough for her to have to fill in for Diana this way. The least Patrick could do was to be mildly pleasant. But his temper, which he usually kept under smooth control, seemed to have reached the breaking point. She had no choice but to follow his order.

It seemed strange to be dressing herself in a costume that she had designed for somebody else. Still, since she and Diana were about the same height, it fit her well enough despite the extra room about the waistline. Once it was fastened, she scanned herself quickly in the mirror, not expecting to see what she did. The fabric, a delicate shade of peach, fell about her with the soft radiance of a sunset, giving her fair complexion an almost luminescent glow. The blackness of her hair seemed like that of a china doll. Double puffed sleeves and a generous trimming of creamy lace, fanciful details of seventeenth-century fashion, made her look entirely different from her usual self. The low-cut neckline revealed a subtly suggestive bit of cleavage and Vicky smiled as she turned around, the yards of satin swaying about her hips.

This dress had originated in her imagination as the epitome of all that was romantic and elegant, and now it was no longer just a sketch on drawing paper but a tangible and lovely reality. Would Patrick be surprised to see her this way, or would his impatient eyes merely dismiss her as a functional mannequin who had been directed to appear under the stage lights? Well, I'll soon find out, Vicky thought as she left the costume room, gently holding up the long, full skirt so that it wouldn't trail on the floor.

There was no one onstage when she arrived,

only the half-finished set, a narrow French house with a small second-story balcony. A flood of lights overhead was so blindingly brilliant that she was unable to see anyone who might be seated beyond her. She narrowed her eyes as she tried to focus. "Where do you want me to stand?" she addressed the darkness as her voice echoed through the auditorium.

"Just go up on the balcony, would you?" shot back Patrick's voice from somewhere in the distance. "Hold it, Franz," he shouted to the technician in the lighting booth overhead. "Wait until she gets up there before you take it again."

Gathering the folds of her long gown in her fingertips, Vicky made her way up the wooden steps that lay in back of the house. She arrived on the balcony, not knowing precisely what might come next, only that Patrick wanted her there. He and Franz Hoffman, the lighting technician, could then try a number of different colored lights on the costume. For a second the stage went completely black before it finally began to glow with a murky hue.

"No, that's a shade too dark," Patrick was calling to Franz. "I want a lighter effect for this scene."

New rays of light traveled to her face, and Patrick's brisk instructions to the technician were the only sounds she could hear. She sighed as she placed her hands on the balcony railing. Nobody liked the tedium of these trial-and-error sessions with lighting, but they were a fact of life in the theater. Besides, the costume was to be used for the play's major love scene, so it was especially important that it be seen in the most flattering way.

At last she stood bathed in a gentle wash of amber that gave the costume an ethereal tint, and Patrick seemed satisfied. "That's it, Franz," he called out. "Just leave it there, will you? Thanks for your patience. It's been a long night, and you can call it quits."

Vicky stood uncertainly on the small balcony, wondering what more her director might want her to do. When her eyes found him in the darkness, she saw that he was reclining low in his seat with his long legs sprawled out in front of him. "Does that mean the rehearsal is over for the rest of us, too?" she asked hopefully.

"Not quite," came the amused reply. "You remain where you are. There's another matter I'd like to go over with you. I know it's late, but it won't take more than a few minutes of your time."

Oh, what now? she wondered with a new twinge of irritation. It was after ten o'clock and she was getting tired. Nevertheless, Patrick was the boss, a particularly demanding one tonight, and she could only wait for his final word.

But as he approached the stage she saw that he was smiling elusively, his eyes taking in the sight of her with decided pleasure.

"Patrick, would you mind telling me what this is all about?" she whispered from her place on the balcony. "Shouldn't we be finished by now?"

"But we've hardly begun." He ascended the stage gracefully and began to stride toward the balcony with light, purposeful steps. Then he stopped below her, speaking not as himself but as Cyrano de Bergerac with a declaration of love to his Roxane.

"Your name is in my heart like a bell shaken by my constant trembling, ringing day and night: Roxane, Roxane, Roxane! Loving everything about you, I forget nothing."

His words were delivered in a spirit of frank delight, and his merry eyes challenged her with such sweet promises that she felt a heady surge of joy. But how foolish this was. He was only playacting, teasing her once again with bewitching illusions.

"Patrick, will you please get to the point, whatever it is?" she said fretfully as she placed her hand on the low, lacy neckline. "This is all a little crazy, you know."

He chuckled robustly, strong white teeth flashing, the stance of his tall body at once proud and full of merriment. "But there's a fine bit of madness in the air tonight, my love. Why not give ourselves to it completely? We may stand on the stage, that most public of places, and yet for the first time in days we're entirely alone. Two long-lost lovers should never let such a rare opportunity be wasted."

Then he was bounding up the steps that led to

the balcony, where he joined her, slightly breathless and filled with glad energy. "Let me speak
to you now in the truest way I can," he murmured as he slipped her hand in his. "Every
man must do so with the gifts that he was given.
These, then, are mine, and I implore you to
listen."

His next words were those of Cyrano, but he
whispered them with such utter conviction and
such a sense of heartfelt sincerity that they seemed
to be his own. Vicky dared not laugh at him
now, and Patrick held her so spellbound that
she found herself falling helplessly into a strange
realm of enchantment.

*"You can't know what these moments mean to
me! . . . until now my words have never come from
my true heart . . . till now I always spoke through
the intoxication that seizes anyone who stands
before your gaze! But tonight it seems to me that
I'm speaking to you for the first time."*

"Perhaps it's true—even your voice is different,"
she heard herself reply softly. That line was
Roxane's, but tonight, as if by sorcery, it had
become her very own.

He warmed to her response, gazing at her
with adoration.

*"I remember the day last year, the twelfth of
May, when you wore your hair in a different style."*
She felt him stroke her hair with trembling
fingers as he continued to speak.

*"Just as a man who has looked at the sun too
long sees red circles everywhere, when I've gazed*

*on the bright glory of your hair my dazzled eyes
see golden spots on everything!"*

Then he was kissing her with searing sweetness, whether as Cyrano or as himself she did
not know and could not care. Yes, there was a
fine bit of madness in the theater tonight. It
came from his hungry embrace, from arms that
possessed her so relentlessly that her half-bared
breasts seemed to melt against him. Soon her
head was thrown back as he began to cover the
hollow of her throat with quick little kisses.

"Oh, please, please . . ." she heard herself
breathe, but her words were not a protest. They
were a plea of longing, testimony to a fever that
was raging far out of control, flashing through
her veins and heating her like wildfire.

When his hands tenderly reached inside the
low neckline of her gown to touch her breasts
under the soft amber glow of the lights, she
could not stop him. And when he began to fon-
dle them warmly, Vicky knew only a strange,
wild ache that threatened to explode within her.
Patrick wanted so much, but she wanted it,
too, with a clamoring rush that she had never
known before. She may have been sleeping
soundly for all these years, but now every pore
of her body was fully awake.

She saw him reluctantly withdraw his hand
from the lacy bodice. "The stage has its purposes,
but this is not one of them," he whispered softly.
"Would you like to go downstairs and change?

After that we can continue the evening in a different way."

Breathlessly Vicky walked with him through the theater basement as shadows flickered across their faces. She had no idea what the rest of the evening might have in store, but she knew she didn't wish to spend it without him. He, too, with his arm resting firmly on her shoulder, seemed intent on keeping her close.

She changed quickly in a kind of trance, and when she left the costume room, she saw that he was waiting for her, a dimpled smile softening the lines of his handsome face.

"Come with me to my hotel, Victoria," he coaxed as he took her hand. "We'll be alone there, and I think we need this time together."

His candor rang a faint bell of alarm in her mind. "But, Patrick, I—"

He led her gently to the stage door, which he opened with a little bow. "There'll be nothing amiss in our sharing a drink or two in my room. I can certainly offer you that, if you'd like, and that alone if you think it best. Whatever you decide, I'd appreciate the pleasure of your company this evening."

"Well, I . . . yes, I'd like to come. For a drink, anyway. I'd like that very much."

The Bell Tower Hotel was only minutes from the theater, so their walk in the warm, dark night was a brief one. They entered the lobby, and Patrick picked up the key to his room with a jaunty greeting to the desk clerk, who didn't seem to notice Vicky's presence. How simple this was, she thought with a secret swell of happiness. People did it all the time, and no one would even think to look at them twice.

She followed Patrick to the elevator, which began to carry them smoothly to the seventh floor. He stood quietly beside her, his upturned profile watching the flashing buttons above them. Then he looked at her and his eyes were so filled with tender gladness that Vicky's heart seemed to turn over in her breast.

The elevator stopped on the sixth floor, its doors opening to let in another passenger, a young man holding a tray and dressed in a navy-blue uniform. He stepped inside automatically before his brown eyes widened with sudden surprise. Vicky stared back at him with a shock of recognition. Oh, my God, it was Bud, her daughter's boyfriend, who worked here three nights a week. How could she possibly have forgotten that fact, only to be reminded of it at this awkward moment?

"Hi there, Mrs. Owens," he said, his eyes still round with amazement as he took in the tall, lean man by her side with knowing curiosity. "Uh . . . are you two going all the way up?"

Before she realized what she was doing, Vicky was pressing her finger on the button marked LOBBY. "No, we're going all the way down," she heard herself mutter as she stared blindly before her. The elevator began descending and finally reached the main floor with a little thud.

She was aware of two pairs of eyes fixed questioningly on her, but Vicky was too embarrassed to look at either of them. "I have to be getting home," she mumbled. "I . . . it's much later than I realized." Then she was marching through the lobby, not daring to look left or right, just wanting to leave the building.

"Would you mind telling me what that was all about?" Patrick asked grimly as he caught up with her at last.

"Patrick, I . . ." Her face flushed crimson, and she turned away from his narrowed eyes. "That bellboy was . . . he's Bethanne's boyfriend, Bud MacGregor. "I *can't* go to your room under the circumstances. Bethanne would be sure to find out, and she'd never let me forget it, not after all the advice I've given her about proper behavior."

"Except that proper behavior for a girl of fifteen isn't the same for a fully grown woman," he remarked caustically.

She looked about her at the darkened buildings along the street. "When all is said and done, Patrick, Ann Arbor is just a small town. People talk here, and gossip spreads like wildfire. This isn't your home, but it *is* mine. I have a reputation to maintain here, and I don't intend to throw it away."

"Spare me the lectures, if you please. And don't try to cast us in the roles of evil villain and unsuspecting maiden. Those parts don't suit us, and you know it."

Their footsteps on the sidewalk provided a brisk staccato of sound, but other than that there was silence. Suddenly Patrick picked a twig from a nearby tree, hurling it with vengence into the deserted street. When he spoke at last, it was in a tone of wry amusement. "It's plain to me that we're two people who have clearly come of age. We're fully entitled to a measure of privacy, but the question is, where to find it?"

Vicky stared grimly ahead of her as she pictured Bethanne, who was probably waiting up for her return at this late hour. "I don't know, Patrick," she replied ruefully. "I really don't know."

Chapter Six

❧

Whenever Vicky looked back upon her brief visit to Patrick's hotel, she did so with a crimson flush of embarrassment. Such foolhardy behavior wasn't her style at all, and she could only conclude that she had been possessed by a temporary madness that had surfaced against her better judgment. Yes, Patrick had a dazzling effect on her, but what of it? He was, after all, just a visitor who would leave Ann Arbor and Vicky Owens far behind him in a month's time. He had never mentioned his future plans, but even so she could not dare to assume she would be included in them. She had a life to live in this small university town. Patrick, on the other hand, would be gone before she knew it. Why should she completely involve herself with him only to face heartache at their inevitable parting?

Meanwhile, the days passed in a whirl of activity. The costumes occupied most of Vicky's hours, and many of them were nearly completed, needing only bits of trim and lace for a finishing touch. Vicky marked off a day on her calendar for a necessary trip to Detroit. There she could find a much wider variety of fabrics than she could in Ann Arbor. In fact, she was used to making such excursions; at least once before each production, she had to drive to the city.

Knowing that it would involve a long and somewhat tiring visit, she planned her shopping tour for a day late in May that promised to be otherwise undemanding. For one thing, Bethanne would be out of town for a three-day class trip up north that her biology teacher had arranged to introduce his students to the flora and fauna of the area. Vicky considered it wryly. Bethanne's interest in biology had become apparent only since she had enrolled in the class with Bud. That, plus the fact that Bud, too, would be going on this little north-country excursion, had turned her overnight into an avid biologist.

Well, it was harmless enough, Vicky supposed, and, of course, the trip would be chaperoned. Still, Bethanne seemed giddier than ever, and as a result her music was beginning to slide. Although Patrick still occasionally mentioned the possibility of Bethanne's performing during the play, he was plainly preoccupied with more immediate concerns. Rehearsals did not always go smoothly, and it was necessary for him to spend a good deal of time helping young David Lang interpret the complex role of Cyrano. Diana, too, was slowing things up by her difficulty with learning lines despite the fact that she was trying. Vicky often saw Diana intently reviewing her lines with Benson Barnett, who was doing everything he could to coach her. Still, she suffered from mental lapses onstage, undoubtedly the result of her growing anxiety. And her profuse apologies to Patrick and her fellow performers, although well meant, did nothing to hasten the tedious, snaillike pace of the rehearsals. No, life in the theater was never easy, and as the director of a troupe of actors who needed constant attention, even nurturing, Patrick certainly had his hands full. Vicky was determined not to add to his troubles.

She was working late one day, seated at her sewing machine as she finished a soldier's costume that was to be worn during the battle scene in the second act. Except for the whir of the machine all was quiet, and she was surprised to hear footsteps at the door.

"Hello, Vicky. I thought I'd check down here to see if you were carrying on in your usual competent manner." It was Patrick. A thin black turtleneck sweater contrasted sharply to his fair coloring, and he looked more striking than ever.

She looked up at him with a smile. "Oh, yes, it's business as usual down here in the costume room."

"I'm glad to hear it. That means I can count on at least one person not to make things more harried than they already are." He grinned ruefully, his tired face bearing the signs of a philosophical humor. "I don't know what it is about this production, but it seems to have an endless number of built-in difficulties, doesn't it? I'm only glad you're not among them."

She smiled her thanks, deeply touched by his compliment. That she could ease the heavy burden of responsibility from his shoulders just a little was a deeply satisfying thought. If only she could also smooth away those weary lines on his face.

"I just wanted to see if things were going well with you," he continued crisply, still the efficient director dealing with one of his chief assistants. "I won't be around this Thursday, so if anything comes up, don't look for me then."

"No problem," she replied even as she wondered where he would be. "I won't be here on Thursday, either. I'm going to Detroit for some trim and fabric I still need."

He moved toward her with a fresh look of interest. "Detroit, is it?" he mused thoughtfully. "There are other places you could go for fabric, you know. How about New York? Don't you think that might suit you better?" He stood quite close to her now, his blue eyes inviting and filled with plans that seemed as promising as they were unclear.

"What do you mean, Patrick? There's no need for me to go all that way—"

"But the fact of the matter is that I'm scheduled to be there on Thursday to appear on a TV talk show. Why don't we go together?" His hands were clasping hers with warm persuasion. "Just you and me with some time to ourselves. It'll be fun, Victoria—a kind of day-long holiday. My plane leaves in the morning, and I'm due back here late that evening. Please say you'll come with me. I'd like that very much."

"Well . . ." The twinkling light in his eyes was irresistible, and his hands sent little flickers of warmth through her whole body. "I don't see why not." She smiled suddenly. "Yes . . . yes, I think I *will*."

She looked forward to the coming Thursday with an excitement she hadn't experienced for a long time. The day promised to be a full and fascinating one, and with Patrick at her side it would be a cause for celebration.

When Thursday morning finally dawned, she was more than ready, her hair freshly washed and dried, her slender figure prettily attired in a new green summer dress with a wide cummerbund and a filmy full skirt. The house was quiet as she waited for Patrick to pick her up. Bethanne had departed yesterday on her own trip, leaving Ann Arbor behind in a flurry of giggles shared by her classmates. Thus, the day would be Vicky and Patrick's, hours of it spent exclusively in each other's company. What a lovely miracle it seemed and, oh, how she was looking forward to it.

Patrick arrived promptly in a taxi at seven-thirty, and soon they were headed toward the airport. He was seated beside her, and his light-weight gray linen suit set off his lean, graceful frame elegantly, its pale color adding shimmering lights to his golden hair. She tried not to stare even as she promised herself to keep this picture of him indelibly in her mind. It would remain there as a special souvenir, one she would cherish in the years to come.

Within a few short hours they had been transported from the quiet, well-ordered streets of Ann Arbor to the frantic ones of Manhattan. Life here moved at a thunderous pace, and the kaleidoscope of sight and sound left Vicky's senses in mad confusion. Even crossing the narrowest street was a challenge, but Patrick instantly responded to her sudden timidity.

"Just take my arm," he offered kindly as a huge truck careened past them. "I'm used to the chaos, and the last thing I intend to do is to lose you in the crowd."

His familiarity with the city streets made him an excellent guide; as he led her along crowded sidewalks, he remarked on points of interest with a spirit of cynical bemusement. He plainly regarded the city with a somewhat jaundiced eye, but he also seemed to appreciate all the riches it had to offer.

Their first stop was at the largest fabric establishment Vicky had ever seen. A costume designer's dream, it consisted of two stores directly across from each other on Orchard Street, both of which were filled to the brim with bolts of material and trim. By the time Vicky finished exploring both shops she had amassed a wonderful assortment of gold brocades, ribbons and lace, all of which were sure to enhance her costumes. Patrick was helpful, too, for he possessed a strong instinct—unusual in most men—about color and design, and he understood what was involved in adapting modern fabrics to the swashbuckling illusions of another era.

"Look now," he advised her as he entwined two pieces of trim, one a shining gold and the other a rich burgundy. "This combination would do nicely for the costume of Comte de Guiche, don't you think?"

His eye was perceptive, and as she agreed Vicky was struck by the sight of his long, slender fingers lightly holding the fabric in place. His were the hands of a lover, she thought with a pang. He touched those bits of delicate ribbon as he would touch his beloved, awakening her body with intuitive warmth and sensitivity. Vicky's heart lurched suddenly, and in her embarrassment she willed herself to turn away. This was nothing, after all, but a pleasant little business trip, so why couldn't her mind respond accordingly?

But as the day rushed by, the business at hand was forgotten in a whirlwind of various pleasures. The TV studio was located near the theater district, and a long line of people stood waiting with tickets for the taping of the show. Patrick, however, bypassed the line, leading Vicky directly to the stage door, where they were admitted by a smiling attendant.

"Welcome, Mr. Wallingford. You're right on

time as usual. From the looks of things out there, I'd say we have a sizable audience waiting."

"A full house at least." Patrick beamed as he followed the man inside and began escorting Vicky down a small flight of stairs. They were led into a cozy area, which Vicky surmised was the TV equivalent of a theater's Green Room, a place for performers and guests to wait until they appeared onstage. Several were already present: a well-known comedian, who looked as droll and sprightly in person as he did on camera, and two others, whom Vicky soon learned were a best-selling author and an Italian racing-car driver. Again she was in far more celebrated company than she was used to, but as Patrick's guest she was instantly treated as a welcome member of the small group. Andy Sachs, the comedian, as eager to perform off stage as on, soon pulled a deck of cards from his pocket and began to entertain her with a series of tricks that left her laughing helplessly.

The brief appearance of Dick Danielson, the show's famed host, was an exciting reminder that the program was about to begin. A dapper, expensively dressed man in his late fifties, Danielson still enjoyed a youthful appearance. He shook everyone's hand, offering each guest a few cordial words of welcome.

"Good to see you again, Wallingford. We always like to add a touch of class whenever we can find it." Danielson's eyes fell on Vicky. "I don't believe I've had the pleasure of meeting your lovely companion," he said in a practiced manner.

Patrick introduced her with a smile, adding that she was here to offer him moral support while he waited to appear on camera.

"I'm sure you'll do a fine job," Danielson told her cheerfully before he darted off, a quick-moving man who was surprisingly smaller in person than he appeared on TV.

The monitor in the room revealed that the audience was being warmed up for the coming show, responding with agreeable laughter and applause to the smooth efforts of Danielson's long-time announcer, Bob James. When a light flashed above the monitor, the show was officially under way, and the atmosphere in the room became charged with a tense air of expectancy as each guest waited to be called onstage.

Vicky stole a glance at Patrick, who was watching the screen with cool appraisal. "Aren't you nervous?" she whispered. "I know *I'd* be. I mean, how do you know what you're going to say?"

"I have a pretty good idea, actually. You see, these shows aren't as spontaneous as they seem." He chuckled as he squeezed her hand warmly. "Besides, how could I be nervous with you so comfortingly at my side?"

She smiled her response, nestling into the plush, nubby cushions of the long blue sofa as she began to enjoy the show. Watching it from this vantage point gave her a new perspective, and she became aware that what appeared to be lighthearted conversation was actually the result of polished showmanship. Everything went well until the appearance of Rico Agnelli, the racing-car driver, whose English proved so halting that even Danielson had trouble maintaining the flow of dialogue.

"That was a rough one," Patrick murmured sympathetically. Then it was his turn. He left the room quickly in a fresh burst of energy and soon appeared on camera.

He was as charming and outgoing in the public eye as he was in private. He soon began to recount several amusing anecdotes of his life in the theater, which the audience enjoyed and which Danielson responded to with a broad smile. With Patrick on the air, the pace of the show visibly quickened, and Vicky could only watch him with admiration. What a gift he had, to generate such an effect wherever he went.

When the show was over, she left the TV studio on Patrick's arm, feeling as though she were floating on air. The day had turned out to be more wonderful than she could have possibly imagined, and it wasn't even over. Their flight back to Michigan was hours ahead, giving them plenty of time to enjoy themselves.

They dined in an elegant but small French restaurant on the Upper West Side. The waiter glided with soundless grace as he obligingly carried a bottle of rare vintage wine to the table for the approval of "Monsieur Wallingford"; it was apparent that Patrick was a frequent and welcome customer. "As a bachelor who lives a few blocks away, I come here frequently," he told Vicky as the flickering candlelight bathed his face with a mellow glow. "I had hoped you would like it, too."

How could she not? Their first course, a dark, almost sweet soup, was fragrant with onions and richly blanketed with toasted French bread and cheese, and the scallops of veal, served in a white wine sauce with plump mushrooms and tarragon, practically melted in her mouth. For dessert they had white chocolate mousse, a pale froth in a tall, chilled glass that came brightly crowned with a cluster of scarlet strawberries. Vicky sat back with a purr of contentment when she had finally finished, pleasantly aware that Patrick's azure eyes had scarcely left her throughout the meal.

"Our evening is still young, you know. What would you like to do next?"

She shrugged dreamily, not really caring how they filled the time ahead. This brief trip had cast a spell on her. Vicky was so enchanted already that whatever they did could only add a shining luster to an already perfect day.

"Perhaps it's time we shared that drink at last. My apartment is close by, and I have some excellent brandy there. Besides, I have some photographs of my country place in Ireland that I'd like to share with you."

He spoke so warmly and invitingly that she could not refuse. Why should she? This was

Manhattan, not Ann Arbor with all its familiar faces. Amid the bustling anonymity of this big city they were blessedly free to go wherever they wished.

Patrick's apartment building, which overlooked Central Park, was a vast stone structure, its sharply peaked gables giving it the air of an old European palace. This was a fitting touch since the Dakota was apparently home for any number of distinguished people. Patrick, of course, was one of them, Vicky thought as she stood beside him in the ornate, old-fashioned elevator. She tried hard not to look too starry-eyed when a famous Broadway composer joined them and spoke with Patrick. Celebrities, of course, had to have a place to live, too. Still, the fact that this building was home to so many of them was a source of wonder to Vicky.

The interior of Patrick's apartment made it even plainer that life in the Dakota was nothing like life in the compact apartment units she had seen in Ann Arbor. The foyer was as large as a comfortable living room, luxuriously papered in a dark, hand-woven grasscloth, with a parquet floor and gleaming antiques that enhanced the general aura of elegance. Beyond that was the living room, high-ceilinged and sprawling, with bay windows commanding a pastoral view of Central Park. Vicky smiled. As impressively large and furnished as this room was, it still had charming warmth, reflecting the man who lived here. Plush leather sofas and comfortable wing chairs of brown and rust were set in cozy, conversational groups. There was also a wealth of fascinating objects everywhere that provided a constant feast for the eye. An old oak armoire in the corner was brimming with a marvelous collection of books, and the scattered Persian rugs were as exquisite as the paintings on the walls. Not knowing quite what to look at first, she looked instead to Patrick.

"This is a wonderful place," she breathed softly.

He surveyed the room with the casual appraisal of one who had grown familiar with it over the years. "Thank you," he said simply. "I like it, too. At least I do most of the time. Now, what shall I bring you from the bar? I can offer you almost anything you'd like."

She was soon curled up on a plush loveseat with a glass of white wine while Patrick, directly across from her, drank his Irish whiskey in leisurely enjoyment. There were a series of photographs on the coffee table between them, and he picked one up with a peaceful smile.

"This is the place I was telling you about, where I spend my summers," he explained as he showed her an old vine-covered stone house set in a sea of grass and brightly colored wild flowers. "It's not far from Tipperary and right in the midst of some of the richest farmland in all of Ireland. To me it's the most peaceful spot on the face of the earth."

The contrast between its rural simplicity and

this sophisticated apartment was remarkable. "Even more than this?" she asked with surprise.

"Oh, much more." He laughed rather cynically as he sought to explain. "The theater is my life, and for better or worse all the noise and confusion of New York is part of that. Still, it wears me down sometimes and frazzles my nerves. That's precisely why Ireland means so much to me. It's the only permanent island of tranquillity that I've found in my busy life."

She watched his face soften as an encouraging thought occurred to her. "Did you ever think of living permanently in Ireland?" she suggested. "There's such a fine theatrical tradition there that I'm sure your talents could be put to good use."

He grinned. "That thought has often crossed my mind. In fact, I recently applied for the directorship of the Erin Theatre in Dublin. It's a position I've wanted for a long time, but I doubt that I'll be seriously considered."

"Why, Patrick?" she asked in a burst of incredulity. The Erin Theatre enjoyed one of the finest reputations, but so did Patrick Wallingford. "I should think they'd want to take you with open arms."

"Thank you," he answered with quiet modesty. "From what I hear, though, they're mainly interested in citizens of the Irish Republic, not in restless ex-patriots like me. Still, I keep hoping they'll change their minds." His eyes left the picture and fell very softly upon her. "Have you ever been to Ireland, Victoria? It's a green and lovely land. It would suit you well."

She shook her head, her eyes glowing. No, she had never been to Ireland, but she would willingly go in his company. At this moment she felt sure she would accompany him to the far ends of the earth if she were given the chance.

He picked up another small photograph, this one of a handsome blond boy in shorts and a T-shirt. "My son, Christopher," he said with touching pride as he shared the picture with her. "He's been away at the Chilton Academy in England, but I'm happy to say that he spends his summers with me." A fond smile tugged at his mouth as he continued. "He's a good lad— far more devoted to soccer these days than he is to his studies, but I'm hoping that will change in time."

Vicky considered the picture as though it were a special treasure. "He looks just like you," she said as something wrenched at her heart. "Except about the eyes. There I think he resembles Diana."

"Ah, yes, he has his mother's eyes."

There was both pain and tenderness in his voice, and in the silence that followed, Vicky recalled those eyes, exquisitely blue and starred by thick, dark lashes. "You still care for her very much, don't you?" she dared to murmur.

"I'll always care for her in a way, Victoria. She's the mother of our son and a lovable, if somewhat muddled, human being." He sighed, leaning forward with a frown. "I'm not sure why, but Diana is like a beautiful child who never grew up. She seems to require a constant nursemaid more than a husband, and though I tried my best for seven years, it was a role we both agreed I was never destined to play. Still, I continue to be concerned about her welfare. I had hoped that the production in Ann Arbor would be a positive experience for her. Now I don't really know. She seems as difficult and as dependent as ever."

Except for the slow beat of the mahogany grandfather clock in the corner, the room was still. Vicky looked down at her skirt, smoothing its soft, green folds with her palm. "I'm sorry," she whispered as softly as she could. Still, in light of the fact that Patrick had apparently needed, but never really received, the love of a real wife, the comment seemed hopelessly lame.

"But enough about me and my cares," he said with a disarming smile. "What about you, Victoria? Was your married life all you had hoped it would be?"

She paused, trying to remember just what it was that she had sought so many years ago. Comfort, peace, and stability had been important, and George had certainly provided those things with unfailing generosity. But something had been missing, she now realized, a certain magic she had never dared to believe could be hers. "George and I had a good life together. Of course he was much older than I, and things weren't terribly exciting." She stopped, a rush of loyalty to George's memory forcing her to phrase her thoughts in a more positive way. "But he was a wonderful person, really, kind and gentle and always considerate. I know you would have liked him, Patrick."

He considered his empty glass as a muscle twitched in his cheek. "That might have been rather difficult, considering that you so plainly preferred him to me."

"No, that *wasn't* how it was at all," she said imploringly as quick tears sprang to her eyes. "Oh, Patrick, don't you see? George was so much like a father to me. That's what I needed at the time. I was just a kid who'd never had a father of her own."

There was a long silence as he placed his glass on the table, his eyes filled with a mixture of understanding, pain, and regret. "All those years . . ." His voice trailed off slowly, and Vicky felt a chill run through her. Patrick was as unable as she to change the past; at this moment they seemed imprisoned by those events, with no choice but to somberly accept them.

"Tell me, then," he said finally, "was there something that I did wrong? Something that I should have done differently?"

It was time to speak the simple truth, as bewildering and absurd as it might sound. "I was never quite sure if you were real," she dared to whisper. "Even now I'm still not sure."

"Oh, I'm quite real," he replied as a weary

smile flickered. "Different from others in your life, but just as real."

His words were spoken with a tinge of bitterness, almost as if his glittering crown of success had grown burdensome, a heavy weight that he accepted in spite of the toll it had taken. Vicky sat transfixed by the proud yet melancholy expression in his eyes. She knew that his life set him apart from the rest of the world, that it had caused him loneliness. Many years of it, perhaps, which had been lost forever. Yes, Patrick Wallingford was very real. At this moment she could not believe otherwise, nor could she turn from the vulnerable warmth she felt in his outstretched hand. Such a strong yet finely boned hand, she thought as she gazed down at it; so very like the man himself.

"Well, the past is over and done with," he mused softly, "so I'll not look back that way again. But the future is another matter. Could I ever believe that you might wish to share it with me?"

She nodded, unable to speak. Yes, she might wish for such a future, although she had never dared to believe that it could ever come about. As she felt his hand tighten about hers he rose to pull her to her feet, and she experienced a heady surge of joy. There was a point, then, at which dreams and reality met. If you wished for something long and hard enough, it could, indeed, come true in a lovely moment such as this.

She was enfolded in his tight embrace. "Oh,

Victoria, there is something in you that soothes me so." She closed her eyes, aware of the rhythmic beating of his heart against hers. Then he claimed her lips in a kiss that seemed to have no end. It was as though he sought nourishment from her, needing her more as his tongue invaded the inner warmth of her mouth to share a silent language all their own.

He pressed her hips to his own, compelling her to feel his nearness—hard, direct, and demanding. Such desire was not for children, but they were no longer young students. This knowledge rang through Vicky like a sudden peal of glory. How sweet and right this wondrous celebration that she had waited for was!

Suddenly he drew away, pausing for an uncertain moment. "Stop me, Vicky, if you think you should," he muttered fiercely. "God help me, but I can't seem to stop myself any longer."

"I don't want you to stop, Patrick. I want to love you, too. Oh, I *always* have," she answered with a certainty that lay deep in her heart.

His face softened with a tender glow as they both smiled, the knowledge of what lay ahead shining in their eyes. They stood for a long moment before he picked her up in his arms, the filmy folds of her dress swaying about them as Patrick carried her through the hallway and into his bedroom, which was shadowed in the growing dusk.

Very tenderly he set her down on the large four-poster bed before he sank soundlessly beside her. His hands traced the contours of her face adoringly, drawing a loving pattern down to her breasts. He fondled them warmly, sending a shiver of tingling expectation through her body.

"Patrick, I . . . I think I'm a little afraid," she whispered.

When she met his eyes, however, Vicky saw that he was as vulnerable as she; a man all too aware that the outcome of this moment was unpredictable, perhaps even harmful. "I know, darling," he said soothingly, with a poignant smile. "I think I am, too, but we won't let it get the best of us." He spoke with confidential warmth, becoming her loving friend who was sharing a very special secret. "There's so much at stake this time and . . ." He clasped her hands in his before he drew them to his lips. "Vicky, I don't want to lose you again."

She closed her eyes, aware of his musky scent and the weight of his strong, graceful body as he gathered her to him. Vicky still felt a tug of apprehension, but she knew she must overcome it. Such fear had driven her from him the first time, and she could not give in to it again; not after all these years, not when she loved him so. She did love Patrick, deeply and completely. To her joy Vicky found that it was a feeling far stronger than all of her fears.

"Oh, so lovely," he murmured as he began to remove her dress, his hands exploring the gentle curves of her body.

"I'm glad you like me, Patrick." Her fingers reached shyly for his shirt buttons, slipping beneath to the smooth skin of his broad chest. "I like you, too." She smiled at this man who had become her dear friend and lover. The last remnants of fear dissolved into a pool of rapt pleasure as she surrendered herself to him.

Contentment dawned with a sweet sense of wonder as their arms reached out to draw each other still closer. This was their time to learn the secrets and delights of each other's body. In that sense they were still strangers, gently seeking to know each other better. Soon enough they reached a tender familiarity as the moments of exploration unfolded, washing over them with soothing warmth.

But it could not remain so for long. A fierce, rushing tide of desire overtook them, and Vicky heard herself moan with abandon. Under the sensitive touch of Patrick's lips and hands, she was being carried along by a whirlpool of intoxicating sensations that swept through her. There was no turning back as this man claimed her with wild, sweet pleasures she had never known before. But she didn't want to turn back; the pleasures were wonderful, carrying her higher and higher, until she was overwhelmed by a convulsion of feelings so complete that it nearly frightened her. And she was not alone. Patrick was with her, and together they hurled to a shattering point of total fulfillment.

They floated peacefully and silently through

the darkness, each reluctant to break the harmony between them. Tightly enclosed in the shelter of his embrace, Vicky felt tears of wonder run down her cheeks. "Oh, Patrick," she breathed with a sob of joy, "that never happened to me before. I thought ... I thought I was dying."

His beloved voice was a reassuring murmur in her ear. "I know, Vicky, I know. It sometimes feels that way, but you weren't dying—you were living. Oh, my lovely darling, welcome to life. I'm so glad we've shared it together."

Chapter Seven

❦

Why should the enchantment of the evening be broken when they could easily return to Ann Arbor next morning? Patrick's suggestion was impossible to resist, and after murmuring slight words of protest for propriety's sake, Vicky contentedly agreed to spend the rest of the night in his arms. How could she not? He held her so tenderly, and the fragrant muskiness of his body was the sweetest scent she had ever known. Tonight was theirs, a secret delight she need not share with anyone. For now the world was safely held at bay; tomorrow's rehearsal was scheduled for late afternoon, and Bethanne was far away on her class trip. This night was a gift, and as Vicky nestled in Patrick's embrace she wished it could last forever.

It didn't, of course, although Patrick awakened her to the new day in another celebration of love that seemed as fresh and as promising as the rising sun. And, like the sun, it warmed her through and through until again, as he claimed her almost fiercely, she reached a throbbing,

dazzling joy that seemed to mark a glad beginning, a renewal in her life.

Then came breakfast in bed, presented by her
smiling lover, who had risen early to get fresh
croissants from a nearby bakery. He served them
on a tray with piping hot cups of coffee and a
single red rose in a vase. They ate in easy silence.
Vicky was propped up on plush pillows, and
Patrick, sitting on the edge of the bed, watched
her with adoring eyes. He seemed to be drinking
in every detail of her, as if he wished to capture
her portrait in his mind forever.

"You're a fair sight in the morning sunshine,"
he mused slowly as the steam from the coffee
curled lazily from the cups. "I thought I'd never
be blessed with the chance to see you at this
time of day."

Vicky smiled radiantly, feeling beautiful in
his gaze, more beautiful than she had ever dared
feel before. If their lovemaking had brought on
this glowing reaction between them, then surely
it had not been wrong. Oh, maybe staying overnight had been a little crazy, but what of it? It
was all the more delicious for that very reason.
Vicky continued to smile, unable to stop herself.
What a glorious way to start the day, and what
a joyful future it seemed to promise.

The time to leave for Michigan came much
too soon, though their special happiness continued through the journey. Patrick guided her pro-
tectively through the throngs at New York's La
Guardia Airport, and when they were seated, he

placed his arm firmly about her shoulders, as if he wished to let everyone know that she belonged to him. Maybe she did at that, Vicky thought in a warm surge of pride and pleasure.

Olivia Street was quiet and shady as the cab pulled up to the house at midday. Except for the tightly rolled newspaper on Vicky's front porch, there was no indication she had not been there as usual. She ambled up the stone walk while Patrick followed, carrying the bags of fabric she had purchased. Vicky noticed a slight fluttering of the lace curtains in the window next door. That would be old Mrs. Carmody, watching the neighborhood with her usual hawklike vigilance. Well, what of it? Vicky thought. It was the middle of the day, and it looked as though she and Patrick had just returned from a shopping spree. Vicky smiled secretively as she unlocked the front door. Well, in some ways they had.

The sight of Bethanne's hiking boots in the foyer caused her to frown. What were they doing here? Vicky was positive Bethanne had taken them on her trip, and they certainly hadn't been here yesterday morning. Vicky bent to pick them up, taking care not to let their muddy soles touch her dress. Patrick closed the door behind him, and she turned to question him.

"How do you suppose these got here? I could swear that—"

She stopped at the sound of footsteps from the kitchen, her breath catching in her throat. Someone was in the house. Patrick's hand on her shoulder was reassuring as he stared over her shoulder, his blue eyes registering a look of surprise mingled with recognition. Vicky spun around. Bethanne stood before them, her pale face a startling contrast to her red-rimmed, tearful eyes.

Vicky stepped forward but a fierce look of anger from her daughter caused her to freeze in her tracks. "Bethanne, what happened? What's wrong?"

"A lot *you* care," came the choked, miserable response. "I've been through the most awful experience of my life, and when I came home, you weren't here." Her voice rose on the last word, as a fresh onslaught of tears prevented further explanation.

Rushing forward, Vicky did the only thing she possibly could. She enfolded the girl in her arms to comfort her. Bethanne, however, would have none of it. She wrenched away fiercely, turning instead to a wall, where she continued to pour out her grief.

"Sweetheart, I can't help you if you don't tell me what it is," Vicky said softly as she stroked the girl's rumpled hair. "I would have come back sooner, but I thought you were away on your trip, so I—"

Bethanne swung around with a vengeance, anger getting the best of her. "Oh, sure. You were counting on getting me out of the way, weren't you? Well, I'm sorry if I ruined your plans, but I couldn't stay on that rotten trip a minute longer.

I found Bud and Heather Hoffstedder making out in the front seat of his car. Heather Hoffstedder, that dizzy little airhead. She's got a million boyfriends of her own, but she wasn't satisfied until she added mine to her list. And Bud wasn't even sorry, Mom. He says he's been feeling tied down and . . .'' She struggled against a new assault of tears, finishing her tale in a strangled, barely audible whisper. "I knew I couldn't stay. Lisa Schildkamp's father came last night to take her home. She had an allergy attack, and they let me ride with them. I just wanted to die, and then you weren't even here when I needed you. Not that you have to tell me where you were." She managed to inject a cutting edge to her tormented voice as she flashed Patrick a bitter look. "It's obvious where you were. You left me alone and took off for the night with your . . . your *Romeo.*"

Vicky remained speechless, Bethanne's words as powerful as a punch in the stomach. She couldn't even deny the accusation. Vicky had been enjoying Patrick's company in a heedless burst of pleasure, never thinking that she might be needed at home. And she *had* been needed. She was the only person Bethanne could possibly turn to for solace.

"Now, just a minute, young lady." Patrick spoke up in a tone of patient but steely calm. "I know you're upset, but you have no right to talk to your mother like that."

The girl laughed hysterically. "Who are you to

be giving me advice? You're as bad as other men—worse, in fact. If you were the last man on earth, I wouldn't listen to a thing you had to say."

He moved forward quickly in an attempt to steady her shaking body, but she dodged him by wildly twisting away. "Don't *touch* me," she sobbed. "Just leave me alone, *both* of you." She tore up the stairs, crying as she went, until she reached her room and slammed the door behind her.

Her hand on the banister, Vicky watched through tears of her own. Bethanne needed her, no matter how loudly she might protest. Vicky had to go to her, offering what she could, to make up for all the long hours Bethanne had spent alone.

"Where do you think you're going?" Patrick's hand was firm, preventing her from ascending the stairs.

Vicky could hardly bring herself to look at him, this fellow conspirator, who had caused her to behave with such abandon. "I'm going upstairs," she snapped. "She can't be left alone at a time like this."

The girl's wailing had increased perceptibly, and Vicky was nearly frantic. Patrick, however, remained maddeningly calm. "I'd say she's giving quite a fine performance," he remarked dryly.

"How dare you say that? She's *my* daughter; you have no right—"

"Vicky, I won't try to come between the two

of you." The strong grip of his hand kept her from leaving. "But before you go up there, I want you to promise me that you won't let her make you feel guilty and hurt you. We did nothing wrong last night. I won't have you apologizing for any of it."

Bethanne's sobs had grown helplessly convulsive. Vicky looked upstairs before she turned to Patrick. "Will you please let go of me? I can't stand here debating with you at a time like this. Besides, you know last night was wrong. It *must* have been wrong, or it would never have ended this way."

Before she knew it, he had joined her on the stairway, catching her shoulders almost painfully. "You mustn't think that, Vicky. I won't let you." She tried to free herself, but Patrick held her so tightly she had no choice but to meet his eyes. They burned with blue flames that seemed to scorch her heart. For a second there was only that; just those eyes confronting her and imploring her for a response that was impossible for her to give.

"What happened between us last night was beautiful, and you must never feel any shame about it," he said firmly. "It had nothing to do with Bethanne—there was no way you could have known she was home. She might want to put you in the wrong, but you can't let guilt destroy what we shared together."

Why was he reasoning with such selfish logic at a time like this? She tried to pull away from him in a burst of fury, but he refused to let her go. Her only recourse was to answer with a logic of her own, the words spilling out with conviction. "If you're trying to tell me that it's fine for me to shirk my responsibility to Bethanne, then you're wrong. I can't do that, any more than you can turn your back on your own son or even Diana. People need us, Patrick, and we can't live our lives as if they didn't exist. It was different eighteen years ago, but we can't pretend any longer that we're living in the past. We both have responsibilities, and they won't vanish in thin air no matter how blind or how selfish you think we should be!"

He reacted as though she had slapped him, his face growing taut and pale before a surge of anger brought new color to his face. "I think you're forgetting something, aren't you, Victoria? Neither of us would be shouldering such responsibilities if you hadn't walked out on me eighteen years ago."

The viselike pressure of his hands on her shoulders, coupled with Bethanne's continued laments, suddenly became more than she could bear. "So it comes back to *that*. You're a fine one to talk about guilt when you've done nothing but try to choke me with it ever since you first came here. Damn it, just let me go. I can't care about what happened between us years ago, not when you've turned everything in my present life upside down."

He released her and slowly backed down the

stairs. "If that's the way you feel, then you give me no choice. I'll leave now, Vicky." He spoke quietly, although his eyes blazed with a sharp anguish that cut into her heart like a knife. "I can see you have your responsibilities to attend to, and I won't stand in your way."

She saw him turn to the front door, his tall body marked by weariness and a kind of proud defeat. Then she was summoned anew by the sobs coming from her daughter's room. Vicky rushed up in a belated attempt to comfort Bethanne, hardly aware of the door closing decisively behind her.

Chapter Eight

❦

Bethanne remained beyond comfort's reach in the melancholy days that followed. Wrapping herself in a cocoon of misery, she ate little and allowed her long, dark hair to droop in stringy tendrils about her pale face. She left for school every morning with the listlessness of a rag doll, returning home in the early afternoon to plop herself in front of the TV in a supposed attempt to do homework. As Vicky watched worriedly she saw that Bethanne was no more involved in her studies than she was in the images on the screen. Instead, she stared emptily into space, the books in her lap going unread while the television provided a jabbering background noise to which she paid no heed. How long she would remain in this trancelike state of mourning Vicky couldn't guess. It would take time for the girl's painful wounds to heal, though, and as her mother she was determined to remain close by.

Vicky was thankful that Bethanne made no more references to Patrick Wallingford, and he dropped out of their personal lives as though he had vanished. Vicky saw him often at the theater, of course—there was no avoiding that awkwardness—but at least he maintained a bland courtesy that enabled them to deal with the work at hand. Even so, Vicky avoided Patrick whenever she could. The very sight of him caused her heart to pound frantically against her rib cage, as if warning her of possible disaster ahead. No, she must not involve herself with this man again; it was risking too much with her already troubled home life.

The knowledge that opening night was only two short weeks away provided some relief. In the meantime Vicky would be virtually buried in the thousands of details necessary to complete the costumes. Afterward, of course, she would be out of danger. Patrick would leave Ann Arbor as suddenly as he had arrived. She and Bethanne could live tranquilly once again, voices from the TV set providing a familiar background noise to their quiet existence. Not a terribly exciting life, Vicky concluded with a sudden pang of emptiness, but a sane one that had proved to be her only choice. Why had she ever dared to reach for more? Life would go on as it had, a bland progression of days and nights wholly untouched by magic. That, of course, was how most lives were lived. Vicky should be grateful that hers would be no worse.

As for now, the rehearsals were finally beginning to take shape, promising a production that, despite the earlier difficulties, had every chance

for success. The actors, including Diana, were
all giving creditable performances, and the elaborate sets were nearly finished, adding their own
special mood onstage.

Vicky, in a brief respite from the costume room
one afternoon, allowed herself to linger in the
auditorium as the run-through of the last act
began. Leroy Leonard, the set designer, had outdone himself. The stage looked beautiful, be-
decked in lush green foliage to create an en-
chanting image of a French convent garden. An
ivy-covered house stood at the head of a winding staircase that formed a graceful trail to the
setting below. Vicky took it all in with delighted
fascination. Yes, life in the theater was often
filled with peril, but moments like this made it
all seem worthwhile.

The rehearsal went smoothly until there was
a sudden, significant silence. Diana, standing at
the top of the stairs for her entrance as the
winsome Roxane, seemed unable to move. She
peered down the winding steps as she clutched
the banister, breaking the flow of the performance to speak as herself and not as Roxane.

"Patrick, I must be a mile high up here. You
know how terrified I am of heights," she blurted
in a panicky rush. "I really don't think I can—"

"Just take your time, Diana. There's nothing
to worry about," came the reassuring reply.
"Walk up and down the steps a few times to get
the feel of them. We won't mind waiting."

Very slowly she placed one of her feet on the

first step, withdrawing it instantly as she wailed aloud. "Oh, no, Patrick, I *can't*. The thing wobbles so much I'm afraid it'll collapse underfoot. It can't possibly be safe, and I—"

"It's completely safe, Diana," he sighed. "I tested it myself several times, and so did Benson. Now, just take one step at a time, and you'll have no trouble at all."

Diana obeyed him hesitantly, only to stiffen after her second step in a sudden state of paralysis. "Oh, no, no, I can't. I'm sorry, but I just can't do it," she lamented, reminding Vicky of an unnerved kitten who had somehow got stuck at the top of a tree.

There was a tense moment of silence as Patrick paused, probably in an effort to gather his remaining patience. When he spoke at last, his voice was even but edged with a note of exasperation. "Yes, you can, Diana. You can do anything you make up your mind to do. Now, please go ahead. We still have the whole act to run through."

Diana remained where she was, covering her mouth in a coy little gesture of doubt as Patrick muttered something under his breath. Suddenly another voice, hale and hearty, was heard from the wings.

"This department of ours has the best carpentry shop in the whole Midwest, so you can rest assured that those stairs are solid as a rock. Couldn't be sounder if I'd built them myself." In no time Benson had joined Diana at the top of the stairs, his stocky form vivid in a bright red sweater. "But maybe a little helping hand is in order," he added with a courtly bow, offering the reluctant actress his arm.

Nevertheless, she remained glued to the spot, unwilling to accept the personal aid of the assistant director. Vicky heard several low moans of frustration from the crew; once again things had ground to a halt, all because of Diana's childish antics.

Benson simply shrugged good-naturedly and, with a characteristic show of understanding, bowed once again. "Well, my fair Roxane, it will be my pleasure to pave your way. Watch me carefully now, and you'll see that you have nothing to fear but fear itself!"

Then, in a light-footed performance, he was tripping down the steps, flourishing one hand above him in a gesture plainly designed to show Diana how undeniably safe the steps were. Benson had nearly reached the landing when he turned around to wink reassuringly at the reluctant actress, continuing downward as he boldly began to take the steps two at a time. He unwittingly stepped into a clay flower pot on the landing and lost his balance completely. Then he was thudding to the foot of the steps, his portly form a spinning, rolling blur of crimson. Diana screamed shrilly while Vicky watched the scene with her heart in her mouth.

There was a mad rush to the stage in the moments that followed. Benson, still lying in a crumpled heap at the foot of the steps, was surrounded by an alarmed group of onlookers, including Diana herself, who had forgotten her earlier fears to rush down the stairs in a distraught burst of sympathy.

"Oh, my God," she kept exclaiming as she twisted her handkerchief in her hands. "I just knew something terrible like this would happen. Benson, are you all right?"

"I'm fine," came the valiant reply with a slight chuckle thrown in for good measure. "Just kind of lost my balance there for a minute, but I'm just fine."

But when he was helped to his feet by Patrick and David Lang, it was evident that he was not fine at all. Trying to stand alone, his florid face went white and he yelped in pain.

"A chair—he needs a *chair*," someone yelled. Benson was soon sitting down, his arms limp at his sides.

"It could be broken, Benson," Patrick muttered in a low, even voice. "At any rate, we can't take any chances." He looked swiftly about him at the faces, most of which were still round-eyed and agape with dismay. His blue eyes fell on Vicky. "Call an ambulance, will you? And for heaven's sake, be *quick* about it."

Shortly thereafter, a moaning Benson was placed in a stretcher and carried down the aisle by two attendants from University Hospital. Franz Hoffman, the lighting director, and Patrick followed close behind them. Before he left for the hospital, however, Patrick turned once more to

Vicky, his handsome face drawn from this latest crisis.

"We've still got a play to do in two weeks, so there's no reason for everyone to stand around wringing his hands," he told her in a calm voice. "I'd appreciate it if you'd take over the rehearsal. The sooner everyone gets back to work, the better things will be. Please don't let me down, Vicky. You look as though you still have your wits about you, and I need at least one person who can be counted on for that."

She nodded, feeling like a trusted captain who had just taken orders from the field commander. Of course she wouldn't let him down. Under the circumstances there was no one else who could carry on. The twittery cast seemed to need all the help and reassurance it could get. Squaring her chin, she met Patrick's penetrating eyes with a look of determination. Their personal lives might be fraught with impassable roadblocks, but right now they had no choice but to overlook them.

Patrick turned to leave, promising to phone the theater with news of Benson's condition as soon as possible. Then Vicky was on her own. The director's notebook in her hands, she took over the rehearsal as calmly as she could. It was unsettling, at first, to think that all this responsibility had landed so suddenly in her lap, but it was only a temporary situation. She soon had the actors in their places, hiding her worries for Benson under a calm appearance.

Patrick's phone call an hour later confirmed her well-concealed fears. Benson had suffered a fracture that would take several weeks to heal. For the time being, he would have to remain hospitalized and flat on his back; the cast and crew must manage as best as they could without him. Unfortunately this would not be easy. As assistant director, Benson had played a crucial role in the production, acting as Patrick's chief adviser and, of course, smoothing things over between him and Diana with his unique brand of diplomacy. Who could possibly be found to take his place? As Vicky nervously considered that, she realized that a substitute would have to be found quickly. Diana required special handling, and a buffer between her and Patrick was essential for everyone's sanity.

The choice of a new assistant director did not remain a mystery for long. "I'd like you to take it on," Patrick told her later as they stood together in the darkened auditorium. She noted the harried look on his tired face. "I know it's a lot to ask of you, but there's no one else to turn to at this late date. Your assistants can finish the costumes on their own, so you'll be free to help me here." He smiled with a hint of dry humor, his eyes holding a challenge she could not refuse. "I'm counting on you, Vicky, but please promise me that you'll keep your balance in the next two weeks. Do you think you can manage that?"

In spite of the serious situation, Vicky laughed

aloud. "You can count on me, Patrick. I'll keep my wits about me, and if it's the last thing I do, I'll certainly keep my balance."

She did exactly that, although her constant proximity to the director was unnerving. Seven short days ago, they had lain in each other's arms as lovers, but how drastically things had changed. Now she was functioning as Patrick's right hand, carrying out his impersonal orders with brisk efficiency and trying to anticipate problems before they arose. One of these, of course, was Diana's fluctuating moods, made all the more troublesome by her rapid gain in weight.

"I've tried to diet, but what can I do?" she asked Vicky desperately one evening as she struggled to zip her costume. "All I have to do is to look at a piece of chocolate and I gain five pounds." Her eyes fell longingly on Vicky's slender waist. "How do you manage to stay so slim? I'd give anything to know your secret."

It wasn't a secret at all, merely a simple matter of willpower. Nevertheless, in the interests of the delicate task at hand, Vicky decided that a little white lie was in order. "Oh, I've gained about five pounds myself in the last month," she sighed confidentially. "It's not really visible, but I know it's there. If anyone should go on a diet, Diana, it's me." She paused, a twinkle lighting up her dark eyes. "Maybe we can diet together. I doubt I can do it by myself, but with you for company it shouldn't be hard. In fact, it might be fun for both of us."

Diana responded with enthusiasm, as Vicky had known she would. The rest was delightfully easy. Vicky stored carrot sticks and yogurt in the theater's small refrigerator to satisfy the actress's constant need to nibble, and she knew her plan would work. Why shouldn't it? Diana seemed to be on the same emotional level as Bethanne, and Vicky hadn't mothered an emotional teenager without learning some adolescent psychology. At home Bethanne was slowly emerging from the doldrums under Vicky's tactful care, and here at the theater Diana was doing just as well. In fact, she had come to rely on Vicky's guidance, as she had earlier done with Benson.

Vicky continued to juggle her various responsibilities with a mixture of poise and good humor. Maintaining a stable home life, supervising the costumes, and performing efficiently under Patrick's expert eye were not always easy, but the challenge was exhilarating. Working with Patrick stimulated everyone, of course, but in Vicky's case it was especially true. There was something about his very presence that had the power to bring out talents and capabilities she never realized she had. When all was said and done, their impersonal relationship in the theater was not so different from that very special night in New York. That, however, was a memory to be banished at all costs, Vicky repeatedly told herself, as she tried to push it from her mind. It had been irresponsible and wrong. Why, then, must it haunt her so vividly, running through her thoughts like a brilliant skein of scarlet?

The Sunday before opening night was blissfully free, the only day of the week without rehearsals. Vicky luxuriated in this bit of unaccustomed leisure, allowing herself to sleep until mid-morning. When she finally arose, donning a short blue robe, she saw to her delight that Bethanne had set the patio table for an outdoor breakfast.

"How about it, Mom?" the girl asked sweetly. "I thought it was time for a little treat. You've been working so hard lately, and it's such a beautiful morning that I couldn't resist. I even went out for your favorite raisin bagels."

Vicky smiled at her daughter and bent to kiss her cheek. "Thank you, sweetheart. This is a wonderful surprise." As she surveyed the wrought-iron table she saw that Bethanne had covered it with a lace cloth, even adding a bright bouquet of poppies for an extra touch of festivity. Adolescence, thought Vicky, was an exuberant, unpredictable stage of life, but at times like this each and every turmoil seemed utterly endearing.

They enjoyed their meal in a mood of cozy well-being, with Bethanne making every effort to be a pleasant companion.

"You know, mom," she mused, "life without men isn't so bad. Who needs them? Just look at the wonderful time we're having together."

Vicky nodded serenely while something tugged at her heart. She gazed thoughtfully at the morning glories, a vivid patch of blue in the sun. Bethanne's underlying meaning was all too clear. She wanted and needed her mother for herself at this point in life. The additional presence of a man, particularly a dynamic person like Patrick, would inevitably absorb Vicky's attention, and could only be a hopeless complication for Bethanne.

The ringing bell at the front door startled Vicky out of her reverie. It's probably the paper boy for his long-overdue collection, she concluded as she scurried inside the house to greet him.

Opening the door, however, Vicky was breathlessly surprised. There, looking rather aloof, stood Patrick.

"Oh," she said abruptly. "I . . . I didn't know it was you." She was painfully aware of her short robe and bare feet. He, by contrast, was fully dressed, his green corduroy jacket a jaunty complement to the highlights in his sun-flecked hair. Nevertheless, his eyes were coolly impersonal, causing her to wonder if he were here on business. "Is everything all right at the theater?" she blurted awkwardly. "I mean, I hope we don't have another emergency on our hands."

Then he was smiling with mysterious charm, his dimples changing his appearance in such an intriguing way that her heart turned over. "I think we've had enough emergencies. Everything's fine, although there is an important matter that needs to be settled. I'd like to discuss it with Bethanne."

Vicky shifted her weight uneasily. The morn-

ing had begun so serenely. "But Bethanne won't
. . . I mean, I doubt if she wants to talk to you,
Patrick. She's still very upset, and I'm not sure
it would be wise—"

"Won't you please let me be the judge of that?"
he asked pleasantly. "Bethanne made a tenta-
tive agreement with me a while ago, and I hope
she won't let me down now. I'd still like her to
play music during the set changes. You know
how tedious those are, and I think the audience
would appreciate a diversion."

"Yes, but under the circumstances—" Vicky
broke off, too flustered to finish. She had nearly
forgotten about the possibility of Bethanne's performing during the show, and now she wasn't
sure how to react. The thought of her daughter
working willingly with Patrick seemed unlikely,
especially in view of recent events. Still, such an
opportunity would provide her with a new challenge and might help to alleviate her bitterness.
"Well, I really don't know," Vicky said softly,
pulling at her robe in a hopeless attempt to
make it cover more of her legs.

Patrick's warm persistence, however, was hard
to refuse. "It's really a matter for Bethanne to
decide, don't you think? I'd like to speak with
her about it if you have no objections."

With a sigh, Vicky led him to the garden.
Bethanne instantly stiffened with glowering
belligerence. She relaxed a little, though, when
Patrick commented that he wouldn't stay long,
and when he explained the reason for his visit,

she began to thaw perceptibly. There were still sparks of anger in her eyes, but he spoke with such a businesslike tone that she didn't bring up the more personal issue that still lay between them. Besides, Patrick charmingly made it clear that he needed her talents. It would be a great help, he explained, if she would play her harp during the three longest intervals of each performance. Her name would be added to the program if she agreed, and he would see to it that she had a costume befitting the colorful period of the play.

Bethanne listened quietly, head held high as though she were a princess about to grant a special favor. "Well, I suppose I will," she consented coolly. "I mean, if it's really so important . . . Besides, I've let myself get a little rusty. This might be good experience for my future career."

Vicky held her breath, certain that this new relationship between Patrick and Bethanne was as fragile as an eggshell and would be shattered to pieces in the days ahead. But although Bethanne was stiff and uneasy during her first rehearsals at the theater, she soon grew openly enthusiastic. In fact, Vicky hadn't seen her in such good spirits since her breakup with Bud MacGregor. It was as though her chance to perform had taken the place of romance in her young life, and she threw herself into her music wholeheartedly. Patrick was quietly supportive and personally selected a costume for her that brought stars to her eyes. It was a gown of gold silk, crowned brightly with a garland of flowers. Sitting onstage with her gleaming harp, the girl looked something like an angel.

Not that Vicky had much time to enjoy her daughter's performances. A myriad of other things claimed her during the frantic week before opening night. She was constantly guiding the cast and crew, offering her assistance whenever it was needed. Diana began clinging like a vine, especially now that opening night was so close at hand. The actress still suffered from panicky lapses of memory, and Vicky patiently coached her just as Benson had before his accident.

The days sped by dizzily, Vicky spinning in time to their crazy tempo. Suddenly there was very little time left. A breathless Vicky suddenly found herself in the Green Room on the evening before the final dress rehearsal. The run-through that night had gone fairly well, though there was still that problem with the props in Act Two to be settled. Vicky sighed, feeling bleary-eyed and wanting nothing more than a good night's rest. She was not alone in her fatigue. Patrick had just gone over twelve pages of notes with the exhausted cast and crew, and now, at midnight, they began drifting from the room, dragging their feet. Vicky rose wearily, looking about for Bethanne. The girl had been here moments ago, but now she seemed to have vanished in thin air. As a matter of fact, the only remaining person in the room was Patrick.

"Have you seen Bethanne?" she asked with a frown on her face. "It's past her bedtime, and I have to take her home."

"She's waiting in the auditorium, sleepy but none the worse for wear. I told her to stay there until you claimed her." Despite the late hour, he seemed full of vibrant energy, spurred on, she supposed, by the smooth pace of the evening's rehearsal. Or was he smiling so gladly for another reason? Before she knew it, he was clasping her wrists playfully. "Don't leave just yet, Vicky. This is a special moment for us, and maybe we should take the time to enjoy it."

Her heart leaped wildly at his touch, and his words held the first personal undertone she had heard from him in weeks. Nevertheless, she tried to dismiss him with a casual burst of laughter. "What makes it so special, Patrick? We've both put in our regular twelve-hour day. I'd say it's business as usual here in the theater."

"Not exactly." His eyes held hers with such an engaging twinkle that she couldn't bring herself to turn away. "Don't you realize that for the first time in weeks we're actually alone? By some miracle of fate our big, happy family seems to have deserted us temporarily. And, strangely enough, I'm not the least bit lonesome. Are you?"

She shook her head wordlessly as intimate memories surfaced in her mind like the rush of spring water. Then she felt the warm impact of his mouth on hers, and his musky scent invaded her senses as he drew her closer. For a fleeting moment she closed her eyes, savoring the sweetness of his embrace once more. Too long, oh, it had been too long since they had been together like this!

Her lips parted at the insistence of his tongue and soon they were fused together, seeking from the other what had been denied them for so many empty days. How sweet it felt to be enclosed in his arms again so possessively, so tightly; how sweet, too, that his hands began to explore the curves of her body, warming her breasts so that they ached at his touch. Pressing her hips to his, he silently told her of his driving need. Something leaped within Vicky as suddenly as a flashfire. What had started as a simple kiss could not be stopped, nor could she keep herself from swaying against him to the pulsing rhythm of her own desire. They were not strangers to each other; they had been lovers, and it was this secret knowledge of each other's body that bonded them together, urging them irresistibly to another point of no return.

She heard him moan her name before his lips fell to her throat, nuzzling it in a fiery frenzy, while his hands reached under her blouse to seek the rounded swell of her breasts.

"Oh, sweetheart. I've needed you so much."

She, too, had needed him, and the warmth of his caressing hands was almost more than she could bear. She was fully alive once more as only Patrick could make her, and when she felt his fingers quickly unfasten her blouse, her senses sang for joy. It was the sweetest of songs, but as her eyelids flickered open she knew it would have to wait for its conclusion. The Green Room was not the place for it, and the theater itself, on this rehearsal night, was jammed with members of the cast and crew.

"Patrick, we haven't been deserted at all," she reminded him as she pulled away in a start, trying hastily to button her blouse. "Bethanne is right outside, and she'll probably pop her head in here any moment."

He sighed, studying her with some vexation. "Sometimes I think you're overdoing this on purpose, Vicky. You don't seem to want to be alone with me for even a minute. In fact, being part of a big, happy family has become your major concern. Tell me truthfully, is that really the way you want things to be?"

She began backing away in a panicky attempt to regain a safe distance from him. "Well, there doesn't seem to be much choice in the matter. Maybe, when all is said and done, that's how things were meant to be." The sudden emptiness in his blue eyes caused something inside her to sink with despair. Painful questions hung in the air, but she didn't have answers for any of them. Vicky turned away sadly, passing through the door to find her sleepy daughter.

Chapter Nine

The evening of dress rehearsal found Vicky dashing madly from one backstage area to another. She just wanted to sit back and enjoy the fruits of her hard work by watching the play, but she was badly needed backstage. There was a problem to be settled with the prop assistant, Kathy Everett, and some of the costumes still needed her personal attention. The largest part of her time, however, was being avidly claimed by Diana Galloway.

"Please, please sit with me during the rehearsal to help me go over my lines," she begged while her face was being made up for a dramatic effect.

Vicky sighed. It was absurd for Diana to make such a request. If she didn't know her lines by now, she probably never would. Didn't she ever think of anyone but herself? The answer, of course, was a resounding no, but this was hardly the time to expect Diana to instantly grow up. Vicky studied her for a long moment. Her enormous blue eyes had been artfully outlined with a dark pencil and highlighted with an effervescent lavender fanning from her eyelids like butterfly wings. At close range her appearance was almost startling, but beautiful in a theatrical way. Nevertheless, underneath all that glitter was an insecure child who desperately sought reassurance. And there was no telling what tricks she might resort to if she didn't get it.

"You know your lines very well, Diana," Vicky began in hopes of calming her. "You don't really need me to—"

"But it's those miserable cues that are giving me so much trouble. Oh, Vicky, you can't let me down now, not when I'm so frightfully nervous." She lowered her voice to a desperate whisper. "Don't you see? If I don't come through this time, it'll be all over for me. I'll be washed up for good."

Vicky's only response was a consoling pat on the actress's shoulder. "You'll do just fine, Diana, but if you'd like me to help you, then I will," Vicky told her kindly. "I still have to check some costume details, but I'll meet you in the Green Room in a few minutes."

Then she was off again, tearing through the basement of the theater, and smarting, too, at Diana's demands. Granted, the actress had a lot at stake, but Vicky did, too. As the assistant director of this crazy undertaking it was her job to watch the dress rehearsal, not sit backstage to play the role of guidance counselor. Patrick would be watching the performance, and her place tonight was at his side, not at Diana

Galloway's. Besides, she wanted to see him, if only to share some time with him. That, however, was not meant to be. More immediate things stood in the way this evening.

When she arrived in the Green Room, Vicky saw that Diana was not yet there. But someone else was, and his unexpected appearance was as welcome as a visit from a guardian angel. Benson Barnett, looking as hale and ruddy as ever, sat there with his cast-covered leg propped up in prominent display on the footstool before him. He greeted her with a broad smile, holding his fingers up in a jubilant sign of victory.

"I made it, Vicky. The doctors tried to stop me, but when I promised that I wouldn't move around, they decided to give me a break." He chuckled disparagingly. "I guess I've had enough breaks for the time being, but wild horses couldn't keep me from this one. The least I can do is lend moral support, and from the looks of things, it's needed as usual."

Vicky embraced him with a heartfelt little hug. Her frantic schedule had prevented visits to the hospital, and she had been able to call him only once. "Oh, Benson, we've missed you so. But you look *wonderful*. I'm glad to see those doctors took good care of you."

"Too good," he groaned humorously. "In fact, I'm beginning to feel woefully guilty about my life of leisure, especially since I left you to carry the load." He appraised her with a disapproving frown. "You've been doing the work of two people, Vicky, and you've lost weight to prove it. Now tell me what I can possibly do to help you tonight."

His concern, as always, was genuine, causing a rush of gratitude to wash through her. "Well, there is something that would be a tremendous help, Benson." Eyeing his cast, which looked too heavy to allow him much comfort in the auditorium, she went on breathlessly. "Diana's in one of her panics. She needs someone to sit with her and help with her lines. I told her I'd do it, but now that you're here—well, there's nothing I'd like more than to watch the play."

"And that you certainly deserve," Benson proclaimed with a smile. "It will be my pleasure to help our leading lady. In fact, Vicky, I think you're letting me off much too easily." Isn't there some grimmer duty that you could assign me?" He patted his cast ruefully. "I'm in no position to be choosy, and you've finally got me where you want me."

Vicky burst into grateful laughter. "Really, Benson, your helping Diana wll be perfect. In fact, it seems the answer to all my prayers." She planted a light kiss on his rosy cheek and dashed off, leaving the backstage world behind her to enter the dark auditorium.

Twenty people were already seated, invited guests as well as friends of the cast. Her eyes scanned the rows of seats, finally resting on the tall, lean figure whose fair hair glimmered from the glow of the footlights. It was Patrick, busily conferring with Franz Hoffman. As soon as he saw her his face warmed with a pleased smile.

"Ah, there you are, Vicky. I was wondering what was keeping you so long. No more trouble, I hope?"

She shook her head. Whatever trouble there might be remained behind closed doors for the time being. Now there was only the quiet joy of knowing that she would be with him in the next few hours. Not a vast amount of time, but it was really all they had and it was precious for that very reason.

"Well, then, come with me," he said invitingly. "I've saved you a seat by my side."

Then they were sitting together, just as she had hoped. Were there really other people here? Their presence seemed dim and far away. In front of her the velvet curtains were about to open for the performance, creating an anticipation that she barely noticed. At this moment she and Patrick seemed to be the only two people in the theater, and his closeness was the only reality she cared about.

He slipped his hand over hers in a sharing gesture that filled her with a warm sweetness. "Has it ever occurred to you, Vicky, that we're the only two full-fledged adults in this entire production?" he whispered with a dimpled grin. "The others are only a lot of children who've had to be coaxed and coddled every step of the way. I want you to know how much I appreciate your help. You've been a blessing to me in so many ways. I'm sure I could never have done this without you."

The touch of his hand warmed her like brandy, and they smiled at each other. How joyful to hear these words of praise from him, and see the look of open admiration in his eyes. Yes, this had been a crazy production, but it had been worth every headache, if only for this shining moment they shared.

Patrick reluctantly withdrew his hand from hers as the curtains parted and reached for his notebook. There was business at hand that neither could afford to ignore any longer. They were here to watch the performance, offering their critiques and spotting any last-minute problems. Vicky sighed. She knew every line of the play by heart after all these rehearsals, and it suddenly seemed like an unwelcome intrusion to have to watch it at all. Why couldn't she just rid herself of the rest of the world to be alone with Patrick instead?

That, of course, was impossible. Before her eyes the first act was beginning, with the fencing match that got things off to a quick start. She settled into her seat, forcing herself to pretend that she hadn't already seen it so often.

The performance went fairly well. Some of the actors seemed stiff at first, loosening up as the play went on, and despite mixing up one line, Diana came through almost gracefully. The costumes looked good, and the difficult battle scene had only one minor blocking problem that

Vicky was able to detect. And then there was Bethanne who appeared discreetly at stage right just as she had been instructed, her music filling the auditorium with sounds of lovely tranquillity at the proper intervals.

"I knew she could do it," Patrick whispered into Vicky's ear. "You see, she's come through for us, after all."

Vicky nodded in proud silence. Bethanne was performing like a trouper, but the best part was the fact that her appearance had been initiated by Patrick himself. As a result, the girl had taken to following him around backstage like an exuberant puppy. Yes, bygones could be bygones, especially in the case of a talented fifteen-year-old who had a full and promising life ahead of her. Vicky felt soft rays of gladness steal through her. What had seemed so hopeless a few weeks ago seemed radiantly possible now. Bethanne adored Patrick, and there was no denying that her mother did, too.

Such feelings, of course, had little to do with the immediate demands of the production, and Vicky pushed them aside. After the curtain closed on the final act, the cast and crew assembled in the Green Room to hear Patrick's evaluation. Since opening night was tomorrow, this would be, for all practical purposes, the last time he would offer his direction. Once the show was launched it would take on a life of its own, surviving, for better or worse, without the skills of its gifted director.

Patrick's mood was warmly congratulatory as he stood before them, one hand thrust into the pocket of his corduroy pants. The rehearsal had gone splendidly, he told them, and the few rough spots could be ironed out with little difficulty. In fact, he was certain that opening night would be all that he had hoped, and he was very proud of every person in the room.

He was rewarded by a sea of shining, smiling faces, although his shrewd psychology was not lost on Vicky. He had deliberately underplayed the weakest spots and, in so doing, had showed them that he trusted and believed in them. Not every director was so generous, but Patrick, who had earned the respect of the whole troupe, could afford to be. Even Diana responded to his words with a rosy glow of optimism. No, there was no one who would let Patrick down tomorrow, especially when he had placed his faith so warmly in their hands.

When the meeting ended, he was called to the lighting booth, and the cast departed for the dressing rooms. Many of them, including a glowing Bethanne, would congregate at the nearby Stage Door Restaurant for a late supper, and their spirits were festive. Maybe too festive, Vicky thought. Giddier than ever, the young actors had disbanded like a bunch of gypsies, leaving costume accessories scattered about the room. That richly plumed hat on the sofa belonged to the arrogant Michael Rowland, and Diana had abandoned her lace shawl near the coffeepot.

Vicky sighed as she picked up these and other items. She had repeatedly told the cast that costumes must be returned to the costume room after each rehearsal for repairs and safekeeping. But they had forgotten, leaving her to pick up while they headed for a merry evening at the Stage Door. She, too, had looked forward to going, if only because she knew that Patrick would be there. From the looks of things, though, it seemed as though she would be cleaning up for half the night.

"You'd think I was a den mother," she muttered, certain there was no one else in the room.

She was startled by a sympathetic burst of laughter. "I know what you mean. Here, why not let me help you? I'm one person who doesn't see you in that role at all."

Standing in the doorway, Patrick was giving Vicky a smile that nearly dazzled her. A moment ago she had felt like a faceless servant, but all at once she was a woman, unique and desirable in those azure eyes that watched her so keenly.

She blushed, laughing to cover up her sudden, giddy feeling. "Oh, you surprised me. I thought you had left for the Stage Door."

"Well, you were wrong. I was waiting for you."

He began to help her, carrying some of the costumes and checking all the dressing rooms for finery that had been carelessly left behind. These he brought down to the costume room, swords dangling from his arms, his face hidden by billows of shining fabric. He even wore two hats on his head, one atop the other, reminding Vicky of a character from an illustrated storybook.

"Are you really there underneath all those things?" She laughed. "Or are you just a walking vision?"

He unloaded his bundles, then reached for the hats and removed them with a flourish before placing them on the old velvet sofa that had been used as a prop in last season's Victorian melodrama. "You see, it's just me underneath all the plumes and glitter," he said with a bow. Then he paused, a slight shadow flickering across his eyes. "I hope you're not disappointed."

He stood beside her in his street clothes, an ordinary man who was, nonetheless, not ordinary at all. "Nothing about you could ever disappoint me, Patrick," she heard herself say, "and the best part of all is that you're real. I'm just glad that you are." She felt herself sway as the brilliant waistcoats and silver-painted swords became a shimmering blur in her eyes.

The vibrant warmth of his arms was real, as was his voice whispering in her ear. "Oh, Victoria, we've come such a long way. Much too far to turn back now. My sweetest angel, I need you so."

Their lips met quickly, filling her with a flood of feeling that was almost painful. Why had she ever kept him from her? Enfolded in his hungry embrace, Vicky was fully alive, heated by a thousand flames dancing through every part of her being. No one else could ignite her so, and as he held her more tightly she felt that she belonged in the shelter of his embrace forever.

She reached for his hair, stroking its softness and moaning in the mounting tide of her desire. Then he was raining kisses on her neck, tipping her head back slightly so that the pulsing hollow of her throat was open to him, sweetly exposed.

A sense of dizziness left her swaying backward, and seconds later she found herself half reclining on the sofa, Patrick's body insistent against hers.

"Ah, Vicky, of my sweetest dreams and memories, I long to love you. I long to love you now."

His voice was a tender whisper to her ears, a poignant line of poetry from a love scene she had never heard before. Perhaps, though, it was being recited for the first time. Surely those words had come straight from his heart. And yet her memory teased her, reminding her once more that this antique sofa had served its time onstage for a drama that had only been make-believe.

"Here, Patrick?" she heard herself breathe in soft surprise. "I mean, it seems like a funny kind of place."

"It's the only place," he murmured as his warm mouth fell to the rounded swell of her breasts. "What better place to bring a dream to life?"

The costume room had always seemed enchanted, but this was one fantasy Vicky had never imagined taking place within its walls.

And yet why not? It was deserted now, as quiet and abandoned as the rest of the theater. Slowly his hands began to unbutton her dress, and she responded with a throb of desire that emanated from the very center of her being, radiating outward in great concentric circles to touch every part of her. Yes, of course, this was the only place, the most perfect place of all.

She watched the fabric of her dress fall away from her, wondering for a dazed moment if she were playing a role before an audience that she could not see. But, no, it was not a role. The fine blue undergarments that Patrick was removing from her body with firm, deliberate hands were not part of a costume. They belonged to her, to Vicky Owens, not an actress, but a real woman who was being heated by a passion more intense than she had ever felt before. And still it mounted, raging into a thousand flames that she was helpless to extinguish.

When her breasts were fully bared, Patrick cupped them eagerly, his breath coming fast against her hair. She moaned, her nipples rising at the tender torment of his touch, and she sought to find more of him, all of him. It was with shaking fingers that she reached for his shirt, another piece of clothing that lay between them. Moments later he was bare chested before her, the powerful breadth of his shoulders and the muscled strength in his arms fully visible to her eyes and to the feverish touch of her hands. For a time she stroked him, raining kisses on his face and throat while he let her continue, a slow smile of pleasure on his face.

But his heartbeat grew fiercer, and soon she was met by a blazing look in his blue eyes that nearly blinded her. Fire had made those eyes more brilliant so that they seemed to be engulfing her like some molten liquid, surrounding her in waves that carried her swiftly to surrender. He crushed her in an embrace that demanded everything, his arms encircling her like steel bands, his tongue invading the deepest corners of her mouth. Together they fell back on the sofa, the hard weight of his body pushing her down and nearly overpowering her. He moaned something into her ear, a ragged sound that might have been her name or simply the urgent, inarticulate cry of his own desire.

Then it was her turn to feel a sense of power. Vicky had never known words to fail him before, but he couldn't speak now, and she felt him tremble in her arms.

Still, he was driven further in his need for her, his lips and hands covering every part of her reclining body until there was no part of her that he left untouched. But he did so with such fierce tenderness that the last remnants of her reserve dissolved completely. How could she stop him now that she was spinning in a pool of pleasures that were too sweet and wild to be abandoned? And how could she stop him when he brought her to a breaking point that seemed to shake her very soul?

"Vicky. My dearest, sweetest love." He finally murmured, his voice gliding to her ears like a melodic song as he enclosed her in his arms once again. The full weight of his body on hers was a glory in itself, and the urgent source of his desire was proof that he could wait no longer. It was then that he claimed her and they became one, united as lovers with their hands clasped tightly together as they entered a world of rhythmic motion. Then all exploded and the world shattered into a million silvery pieces as they held each other tightly.

It was as though a storm had raged through them, and now, in its aftermath, they lay still in each other's arms, savoring their nearness for a measureless span of time. Slowly the room took on a sharper focus as a myriad of details surfaced clearly in her mind. Suddenly Vicky heard herself laugh softly in a small burst of delight.

"And I thought I knew everything about dress-rehearsal nights. I guess I was wrong. Life in the theater is full of surprises, isn't it, Patrick?"

"Always," he assured her with a warm smile, his hair falling in gleaming disarray onto his forehead. "Fortunately this was one of the happier ones. Oh, Vicky, if only you could spend the night with me." He sat up slowly with a sigh. "But I seem to recall something about a gathering at the Stage Door. I suppose we ought to go, if only to put in an appearance."

"We probably should," she agreed. There was also Bethanne to think about; she would surely be wondering what had delayed her mother. Vicky sat up, reaching for her clothing, which had fallen to the floor along with some of the lavish stage hats. For a moment she stared down in bewilderment. Which were the costumes of the make-believe world, and which belonged to her?

"There are dress rehearsals and then there are undress rehearsals," she said to Patrick in a wistful attempt at humor, as reluctant as he to have to break away so soon. "But no matter what, there always seem to be obligations standing in our way."

He grinned wryly. "Well, I think we've done a fine job of meeting most of them. Besides, things won't always be like this for us. By tomorrow we should know for sure." He smiled while he reached for his shirt, a mysterious twinkle lighting his eyes.

"What do you mean?" she asked. "Tomorrow's opening night but—"

"It has nothing to do with opening night," he said as he rose from the sofa, briskly tucking his shirt into his trousers and regaining his air of impeccable elegance. "You see, the people at the Erin Theatre have promised to call me tomorrow, so my future plans should be clear by then."

She smiled at him joyously. "Patrick, that's *wonderful*. Oh, I knew they'd choose you for the job. Didn't I *tell* you—"

"I appreciate your confidence, Vicky, but they haven't really offered it to me, at least not yet."

His tone was solemn, although his eyes, she saw, were filled with hope. "For all I know, old Liam McKenna will be calling to convey his condolences. They may have chosen someone else, you know."

"No, they haven't. They've chosen you, Patrick, because you're the only person for the job. You just wait and see. Tomorrow you'll know how right I am."

He took her hand in his and squeezed it before they left the costume room in a buoyant, optimistic mood. Supper at the Stage Door was fun, although Vicky was too excited to taste anything. When she finally left, taking Bethanne home for a well-deserved night of rest, she found she was unable to sleep. Lying in bed, Vicky was enchanted by visions that floated before her eyes.

"Have you ever been to Ireland, Victoria?" Patrick had asked that fateful night in his apartment. *"It's a green and lovely land. It would suit you well."*

Chapter Ten

❧

Vicky spent the day of opening night in a strange kind of limbo. There were no meetings scheduled, providing a quiet spell of time that was supposed to serve as a peaceful breather for everyone. Still, the anticipation of what lay ahead made it hard to relax. Vicky did her best, strolling downtown on some minor errands and then making an elaborate ritual of doing her nails. The bright spring morning somehow turned into afternoon. Time seemed to be moving for her, but at such a snaillike pace.

As the hours inched along she tried to keep herself from dwelling too deeply on Patrick's words of the night before. If he did go to Ireland, what might that have to do with her? Unless he had meant ... Hastily she forced herself to examine the daily mail, a couple of bills and a flyer from a local lawn-care service. She must not set herself up for a crushing blow of disappointment. What had seemed so sweetly tangible last night may have been the result of her own wishful thinking. In fact, ever since Patrick's arrival in town, she could scarcely tell where her wishes left off and the real world began. She was sure to find out later, if only she could wait.

The interminable day finally accelerated when Vicky reached the theater. The two hours before curtain time saw a beehive of activity backstage. The makeup and costume rooms overflowed with actors, and the buzzer at the stage door sounded constantly. Flowers were being delivered, most of them for Diana, and the air pulsed with excitement. Small repairs and adjustments kept Vicky busy with the costumes. She saw Patrick only once, engaged in a hurried conversation with Diana.

"Meet me in the auditorium, Vicky," he called to her as three half-dressed actors dashed past him. "We'll be sitting front row center."

She nodded breathlessly before he turned away for something that needed his last-minute attention. Vicky, too, had her hands full. The buttons on Michael Rowland's jerkin had to be fastened more securely, and one of the soldier's swords seemed to have vanished mysteriously. In fact, the longer she remained in the costume room, the more entangled she became in these minor crises. When David Lang came darting into the room five minutes before curtain time, she knew she would be late.

"You're going to kill me," he told her sheepishly, "but Mike Rowland and I were clowning around a little, and I'm afraid I've torn my costume."

Oh, would this ever end? Her eyes went quickly to his baldric, the band around his blue tunic that served as a sword holder. It was ripped at the seam and hung limply, the final straw that would prevent her from getting to Patrick's side on time. But the costume needed her attention. In his role as an elegant cavalier, David couldn't be sent onstage looking like a vagrant, and she had no choice but to stitch the material quickly, promising to reinforce it during the intermission.

When she finished, the performance had been under way for a full ten minutes. Cyrano de Bergerac had not missed his entrance, but Vicky Owens had certainly missed hers, she thought wryly. She stole into the auditorium, where she reluctantly seated herself in the back. At this point she would be too conspicuous making her way down the long aisle to the front row. She would have to content herself here.

It wasn't long, however, before she found herself entranced by the play. Last night it had seemed almost sluggish, and she had watched it as a disinterested observer. But tonight—oh, tonight it took on a magic all its own. It wasn't only that Patrick's influence was evident in every scene, but the cast had finally risen to vibrant new heights before the eager eyes of the audience. Vicky wasn't altogether surprised. She knew from past experience that actors often needed the presence of a live audience in order to give their best performance. As a result, they were creating a spell of total enchantment for the audience this evening.

Diana's entrance as the lovely Roxane was hailed by enthusiastic applause. She was, of course, a well-known professional actress with a good reputation, and she did not disappoint her fans. She presented a vision of fragile, ethereal beauty, and her appearance prompted several people in front of Vicky to exchange whispered words of admiration.

"Isn't she stunning? Even more than she is in her pictures."

"All that and talent, too. Just wait till you hear her speak."

Vicky had to stifle a sudden urge to giggle. For weeks she had been a firsthand witness to Diana's personal weaknesses, and it was hard to imagine that they were not apparent to everyone. But, of course, these strangers didn't know about her childish foibles and outbursts. All they saw onstage was a beautiful veneer, proof that the illusions of the theater were as artful and deceptive as ever.

But there was more to it than mere make-believe. As slender and exquisite as she now appeared, Diana was delivering a superb performance. Vicky studied her in fascination. The woman really was an actress of remarkable ability. Why had she never realized it before?

Maybe she had been too bogged down in details to see the simple truth. Diana's voice, especially onstage, was as clear and sweet as ringing bells, and she moved with the grace of a dancer. Moreover, her characterization of Roxane was

captivating. She was, in fact, succeeding in showing her own best traits to her audience, and
Vicky could only be happy for her. This performance represented a personal triumph in so
many ways, living proof that Diana was still,
after all, an outstanding actress of the modern
stage. Surely she would gain new confidence
from this experience, showing even Patrick that
she was worthy of serious consideration.

Vicky shifted in her seat, aware that her palms
were growing uncomfortably sticky. She did not
begrudge Diana her success, but she watched
her with growing trepidation. All eyes were on
the stage. Patrick's were, too, observing what
was so strikingly visible from every angle. Diana was an artist. Patrick had loved her once.
Was it impossible that he could love her again?

Vicky was not alone in this speculation. As
she made her way into the crowded lobby during intermission, she could not help but over-
hear comments from several people in the crowd.

"Galloway and Wallingford still make quite a
team, don't they?" remarked one man. "They're
putting on a rousing show, far better than anything my ex-wife and I could ever manage to do."

"Well, you obviously haven't been doing your
homework, Bertram," came the wry response.
"If you had, you'd know they're still quite taken
with each other. The word is that they'll be
living in wedded bliss again before too long."

Vicky felt her heart tighten even as she tried
to prevent herself from jumping to conclu-

sions. No, that's not the way things are at all, she felt like shouting. Such rumors were nothing but idle chitchat. Why then, was her head pounding almost painfully, and why did she feel so unnerved?

Suddenly she heard her name being called from the back of the lobby. It was Patrick's voice, and as she weaved her way through the crowd she saw that he was not alone. In fact, he was in the center of a dignified group of university officials, including Dr. Samuel Chamberlain. But in her eyes the others faded into insignificance. There was only Patrick, tall and smiling, his hair even more golden against the moss-green tweed of his suit. It was a color that became him, Vicky thought as her heart seemed to stop beating. And well it should, of course, for it was the color of Ireland.

"Vicky, where have you been?" he asked with concern, reaching for her hand and squeezing it as long as their public situation allowed. "I was hoping you'd sit with me."

"Sorry," she managed to whisper as someone pushed past her. "Something came up backstage, and I—"

She didn't have a chance to finish. She was interrupted by the inevitable round of amenities, led by the approving Dr. Chamberlain. He was greatly enjoying the performance, he explained, and the costumes were a credit to their designer. The cast, too, was doing an excellent job, highlighted by the considerable talents of Miss Galloway.

"I'm most impressed," Dr. Chamberlain commented in his reserved, courteous manner. "I knew she was good, of course, but I wasn't prepared for such a stellar performance."

Patrick's face softened with a look of diffused pleasure as he dipped his head in acknowledgment. "I won't contradict your kind words, Dr. Chamberlain. Diana does seem to be her old self this evening. I'm proud and delighted, but, of course, we all feel that way."

He turned to Vicky, who managed to respond with appropriate words of agreement that tasted like cardboard in her mouth. Yes, Diana was the star of the evening, an actress who was enjoying her rightful place in the limelight. Why on earth should this perfectly logical state of affairs seem almost menacing?

Flickering lights indicated that the next act was about to begin. "Vicky, I must speak with you privately later tonight." Patrick's eyes were graver than they had ever looked, full of unspoken secrets. "Promise that you won't keep eluding me all evening. This matter needs . . . well, it will take a bit of explanation, I believe." He smiled almost uneasily, as though he anticipated something uncomfortable.

"Is it about Ireland, Patrick?" she heard herself ask, trying to ignore the warning signals clamoring in her mind.

"Well, yes, in a way. But it concerns other things, too. I can't tell you here, and backstage will be a madhouse in the next few hours." He paused, wrinkling his brow in consternation. "Look, Chamberlain has insisted on taking me out for a drink after the performance, but I'll be at the party right after that. It may not be the best place, although I think we'll be able to find a little corner to ourselves for a spell. You will wait for me, won't you?"

His eyes held her urgently with a hint of something so overwhelming that it nearly frightened her. "Yes, of course I'll wait," she managed to reply. Bodies pressed against her as the swarming crowd made its way back into the auditorium. Patrick was claimed by Dr. Chamberlain, who accompanied him inside, while Vicky remained where she was. That cursed baldric on David Lang's costume! She had promised to check it during intermission, and she had almost forgotten. Dashing backstage, she resumed her work in the costume room.

And so it went throughout the performance. Whenever she could, Vicky tiptoed into the back of the auditorium, even managing to watch most of the last act without interruption. The final love scene was emotionally stirring, and when it was time for the curtain call, the audience rose to its feet to hail the radiant Diana. Vicky applauded with them, for she had been moved to tears by this sad, sweet tale of unrequited love.

Diana's performance had been flawless—poignant and shining with that undeniable aura that lifted her magically into the realms of pure artistry. Graciously receiving the acclaim, Diana looked both proud and humble. She had managed to overcome all sorts of personal difficulties to reach this moment in her life, and she seemed well aware of it. Nor was the meaning of the moment lost on Vicky. She had worked too closely with Diana not to realize that an unexpected miracle had finally taken place.

The adulation continued in the Green Room, where the actors were congratulated by friends and admirers. Surrounded by a smiling host of them, Diana was deeply moved, her lovely face streaming with tears of joy.

"She deserves all the praise in the world, of course, but you do, too, Vicky. Try not to feel too overshadowed tonight. Your efforts have certainly been appreciated by everyone."

Benson sat on the sofa, his injured leg propped up stiffly. He smiled kindly before he gave Vicky's hand a friendly squeeze. "We all have a lot to celebrate tonight, my dear, and I certainly hope you will be at the cast party. Wallingford has accepted that directorship in Ireland, so you'll want to say good-bye to him. He especially wants to speak to you, Vicky. In fact, he told me he's been so pleased with your work that he's thinking of recommending you for a promotion. And, needless to say, a recommendation from Pat Wallingford will go far with the powers that be in Ann Arbor."

Vicky's face went white, although her sudden loss of color was genially misinterpreted by Benson as a case of delighted amazement. "You see,

Vicky," he explained with a knowing little chuckle, "even those of us who quietly labor backstage can have our moments in the sun. You shouldn't look so astonished. In your case, I can assure you, it's highly deserved."

Something inside her was plummeting swiftly, and Vicky clutched his hand as though it were a life support. "Didn't I tell you that we all have a lot to celebrate?" he continued with a broad wink. "And that's not all." It seems Cupid has been busy backstage, so there'll be a special little announcement at the party, too. Not that it should come as a great surprise, but the happy couple want to share their good news with everyone."

Suddenly his ruddy face, so animated with smiles and goodwill, was the last thing that Vicky could bear to see. She turned away, muttering an excuse, and began to push her way through the crowd in a desperate search for quiet.

But there was no quiet to be found backstage. As Vicky groped through hallways and corridors she was met by a sea of faces, swimming before her eyes as if they were all underwater. Surely Benson could not have meant what she thought he did. It was far too terrible to be true, and she mustn't blindly accept it. She had to know the whole story. There must be another side, and only Patrick could tell her. He did care for her; he *must* care for her. What else had their time together meant? She tore through the building trying to find him. Her fate would hang on his words, and her heart, too.

Finding him in the frantic aftermath of opening night wasn't easy. She was stopped by several actors who needed directions to the party, and then Bethanne collided against her on a mad dash down a stairway.

"Oh, Mom, the audience *loved* it," the girl exclaimed with an exuberant hug that nearly knocked Vicky over. "And Patrick is so pleased. He told me I have wonderful things in store for me. That's exactly what he said. Oh, Mom, he's super, isn't he? Aside from Daddy, he's the most terrific man I've ever met." She was jumping up and down in her excitement before she restrained herself with a delighted little giggle. "But I guess you think so, too."

Vicky did not answer, but patted her daughter distractedly on the back. "Do you know where he is, Bethanne? There's something I have to ask him."

"I think he went to the dressing rooms to congratulate some of the actors. At least, that's where he was going when I saw him."

Vicky didn't wait. The dressing-room area would afford no more privacy than she and Patrick had known for the past six weeks, but that couldn't be helped. She had to see him now, before her tightly coiled nerves shattered completely. Reaching her destination in a few breathless moments, she could hear Patrick's deep voice carrying melodiously to her ears. She followed the sound with her heart in her mouth, finally stopping outside a doorway.

But the scene inside the little room was too intimate and tender to be interrupted. There, amid bouquets of brilliant roses and a host of messages from well-wishers, stood Patrick and Diana, their arms wrapped about each other in a warm embrace. Diana's face was more radiant than ever, her eyes closed as she listened to Patrick's loving words of praise.

"You were everything I'd hoped you'd be, darling, and so much more," he said as he gently stroked her cascade of golden curls. "Both of us are off to a brand-new beginning, and the future will be far better than we ever dreamed possible."

Their bodies, silhouetted against the scarlet flowers, fused together as though they were no longer two separate individuals but one person. They belonged to each other, after all. Vicky watched for a horrified moment, knowing beyond all doubt that she had found the answer she sought. It would remain sharply imprinted in her mind for the rest of her life, an indelible portrait of two people who had found their happiness together while hers had ebbed slowly and surely from every ounce of her being. She froze for a second, then turned and rushed down the hall.

Chapter Eleven

Long after the others had left the theater, Vicky remained behind in the costume room, a solitary figure among the shining brocades and jeweled gowns. This place suddenly seemed comforting, a sanctuary for her raw and painful wounds. It was familiar, of course, but it offered much more than familiarity. Here, at least, the illusions of the theater could not be destroyed. The curtain had fallen on the play's final act, but all the trappings of grandeur and loveliness continued to shine right here at her fingertips. They wouldn't vanish with the night, nor would they ever betray her. In this room her fondest fairy tales could reign supreme, unharmed by the harsh forces of the real world.

She had to face that world again, but the thought caused fresh tears to stream down her face. No, not yet; it was too soon. The party loomed before her like a menacing nightmare, and she knew she couldn't go there. She would simply have to return home, her footsteps echoing along the deserted streets as she gained distance from the site of the evening's festivities. The others might have every reason to celebrate, but she had none at all.

Fool that she was, she had dared to believe that tonight her dreams would come true. Well, they wouldn't, any more than that gilt-edged pendant on the table would miraculously turn to gold. Patrick's "love" for her had been just like that—a dazzling imitation. He had been nostalgically amused by her for old times' sake, and he was undoubtedly grateful for all her hard work.

His true feelings, however, had never gone beyond that. He had merely toyed with her during his visit to town, waiting all the while for Diana Galloway to reclaim her inimitable place in his heart. Now that she had, his little interlude with Vicky Owens had plainly run its course. That was what he meant to tell her tonight, Vicky thought, adding a pat on the back and the promise of a job recommendation to soften the blow. Well, thank God she wouldn't be there to listen. Nor would she bid the happy couple a fond farewell before their departure for Ireland. Let them go with everyone else's best wishes. They certainly didn't need hers.

She had, ironically, done more than her share to bring about their blissful reunion. It had been she who had coached Diana, helping her patiently with her lines and tactfully helping her lose almost eleven pounds. But the results of these efforts had been far different from what

Vicky had imagined. Diana had performed superbly, and her appearance, in costumes designed and created by Vicky herself, had captivated Patrick all over again. Yes, Diana's comeback was a triumph in countless ways, with Vicky all but handing her, like a gift-wrapped package, into Patrick's waiting arms. Those arms would never hold Vicky again, and she felt a fresh pang of sorrow. They had been offered as the briefest kind of haven, but she had wanted to remain there forever.

She was weeping soundlessly when she heard footsteps in the hallway; she tried to collect herself as best she could. That would be someone from the maintenance staff, informing her that the time to leave the theater was long past. Wearily she reached for her raincoat and purse, knowing that the sanctuary of the costume room was hers no longer. But the person who appeared in the doorway was the one she could least bear to see. It was Patrick, his hair slightly windblown, his demeanor suggesting the frenzied, impatient air of a man who had been searching.

"Vicky, what are you doing in here? You were supposed to meet me at the party. Don't you remember?"

His hands dug into her shoulders as though he might shake her, and Vicky had the awful feeling she had been exposed without mercy. He had been stalking her, finally uncovering her in this tearful state in which her heartbreak was painfully evident. She should hate him for such cruelty, but as she met his sky-blue eyes she found that she could not. Love might be only a game to him, but how beautifully he had played it. With him she had known her first taste of ecstasy, a gift that was no less sweet now that she had lost it.

"For God's sake, Victoria, I want an *answer* from you," he said demandingly. "You knew I wanted to speak to you, yet you've been deliberately running from me all night."

Somehow she managed to free herself from his steel grip, turning her back so that she wouldn't have to face him. "I didn't meet you at the party because I knew what you were going to say. Benson told me earlier. Hearing it from him was enough. I . . . I didn't want to have to hear it from you, too."

. "How could Benson possibly . . . Vicky, tell me what he said to upset you so." His tone was still impatient but mixed now with a note of sympathy that was even harder to bear.

She fixed her head at a proud angle, trying, at least, to keep the shabby remnants of her pride intact. "He told me that you got the directorship in Ireland—I suppose I should congratulate you for that—and that you would recommend me for a promotion here. And then he said—" Her voice broke before she was able to continue in a strangled whisper. "He said there would be a wedding announcement at the party that everyone had been expecting. That's good news, of course. I . . . I hope that you and Diana will be very happy."

Her body had gone limp from the effort of repeating Benson's words, and when she felt Patrick's arms about her in a sheltering embrace, she could only collapse against him helplessly. "Oh, darling, you should never get your news from a secondhand source. Why didn't you come to *me*?"

The last shreds of her pride dissolved with his nearness, and his hands, gently stroking her hair, were too comforting to be resisted. "I did, Patrick," she whispered, "but you were with Diana in her dressing room." This uttered, she buried her face against his shoulder and let her tears fall.

He held her for a long moment, softly rocking her as if she were a child. Then he began to speak, and surprisingly, his low voice took on a hint of merriment. "Well, you heard only a small part of the news. There *was* a wedding announcement at the party, but it had nothing to do with me. It was made by Benson and Diana. They plan to be married in three weeks."

Vicky looked up through her tears. "If that's supposed to be a joke, Patrick, I don't think it's funny."

"Oh, but it's not a joke," he said with a reassuring smile. "It seems that Benson fell madly in love during the course of this crazy production. We were too caught up with other things to see what was so clear to everyone else, but it's true, Vicky. If you think about it, you have to admit that it makes a kind of wacky sense. Benson is the kind of man Diana has always needed. He has the patience of Job, and he fairly worships the shaky ground she walks on." His lips brushed her forehead lightly. "If he can just manage to keep his own balance in the future, there's no reason why they shouldn't live a long and happy life together."

Vicky laughed giddily as the image of Diana and Benson as a married couple made its impact. They were complete opposites, but maybe that was where the attraction lay. Diana would bring sparkle and elements of madcap uncertainty to Benson's tranquil life, and he would be the jolly, dependable father figure she seemed to require. Oh, yes, Vicky realized as she succumbed to a fresh peal of laughter, they would be perfect for each other. In fact, theirs most surely would be a match made in heaven!

"You see, Vicky, this has turned out to be a night for joy, not tears," Patrick was saying in his softest voice. "When you saw me in Diana's dressing room, I was congratulating her and wishing her well. She'll be staying in Ann Arbor to liven up the theater department, but I'm leaving for Ireland. At least you were right about that. And you were right about something else, too." He paused, then his words came with increasing significance to her ears. "That promotion is yours if you want it. I don't relish working at the Erin Theatre without a costumer of your many talents."

He kissed her eyelids, and a spring of hope

burst within her, vying with the doubts that still lingered. "But, Patrick, I'm not sure I . . . I can't just pick up and go unless—" She stopped uncertainly, too dazed to go on, not daring to hope for anything more.

"I know, darling, and that's what I had to talk to you about." He drew a long breath, his eyes enveloping her with tender radiance. "Victoria, I love you and I need you. You're my lovely island of tranquillity in this topsy-turvy world. You're also that rare thing in the theater—a beautiful woman who doesn't think the world revolves around her alone. I'm asking you to marry me, don't you see? I want you at my side, where I can love and cherish you for the rest of our lives."

Vicky closed her eyes against an overwhelming rush of joy as she swayed slightly against him. "Oh, Patrick, yes, I'll marry you. I'd go to the ends of the earth with you. I love you, too, more than—"

But her words were interrupted by his ardent lips, claiming her in a kiss that warmed her to her very core. Patrick's arms tightened around her, and her body melted into his.

Moments passed before he drew away, his mouth nuzzling her tousled black hair. Then a practical thought began pushing its way through her euphoria. "Oh, Patrick, I almost forgot. Bethanne has her schooling here, and we—"

"I was wondering when you'd remember that," he murmured with a twinkle in his eyes. "I haven't forgotten a thing. Bethanne would be delighted to attend the London College of Music—she told me so after the performance—so you'll just have to let me pay her tuition. She deserves the chance, and she'll be close enough to visit us in Dublin on her free weekends. The rest of the time it'll be just you and me, which, I confess, has been an ulterior motive of mine since I first laid eyes on you." Then his most charming smile widened on his face as his manner grew playful. "But I really wouldn't want you to rush blindly into anything. Tell me honestly, do you think you could be happy with that kind of life?"

She nodded silently, content to let her glowing eyes speak for her. This was no fool's fantasy that would vanish as quickly as the mercurial illusions of the stage. The feel of his kisses on her flushed face was very real, as real as the silken strands of his hair and the delightful, musky scent of his skin. Patrick was hers to love forever, a truth that was reinforced by the sound of his beloved voice as he murmured her name. No, her senses assured her, she was not dreaming. Her wish had been granted, filling her arms and her life with a golden reality.

RAPTURE ROMANCE
BOOK CLUB

Bringing You The World of Love and Romance With Three Exclusive Book Lines

RAPTURE ROMANCE • SIGNET REGENCY ROMANCE • SCARLET RIBBONS

Subscribe to Rapture Romance and have your choice of two Rapture Romance Book Club Packages.

- **PLAN A:** Four Rapture Romances plus two Signet Regency Romances for just $9.75!

- **PLAN B:** Four Rapture Romances, one Signet Regency Romance and one Scarlet Ribbons Romance for just $10.45!

Whichever package you choose, you save 60 cents off the combined cover prices plus you get a FREE Rapture Romance.

"THAT'S A SAVINGS OF $2.55 OFF THE COMBINED COVER PRICES"

We're so sure you'll love them, we'll give you 10 days to look over the set you choose at home. Then you can keep the set or return the books and owe nothing.

To start you off, we'll send you four books absolutely **FREE.** Our two latest Rapture Romances plus our latest Signet Regency and our latest Scarlet Ribbons. The total value of all four books is $9.10, but they're yours **FREE** even if you never buy another book.

To get your books, use the convenient coupon on the following page.

YOUR FIRST FOUR BOOKS
ARE FREE

Mail the Coupon below

Please send me the Four Books described **FREE** and without obligation. Unless you hear from me after I receive them, please send me 6 New Books to review each month. I have indicated below which plan I would like to be sent. I understand that you will bill me for only 5 books as I always get a Rapture Romance Novel **FREE** plus an additional 60¢ off, making a total savings of $2.55 each month. I will be billed no shipping, handling or other charges. There is no minimum number of books I must buy, and I can cancel at any time. The first 4 FREE books are mine to keep even if I never buy another book.

Check the Plan you would like.

☐ **PLAN A:** Four Rapture Romances plus two Signet Regency Romances for just $9.75 each month.

☐ **PLAN B:** Four Rapture Romances plus one Signet Regency Romance and one Scarlet Ribbons for just $10.45 each month.

NAME _____
(please print)

ADDRESS _____ CITY _____

STATE _____ ZIP _____ SIGNATURE _____
(if under 18, parent or guardian must sign)

RAPTURE ROMANCE

This offer, limited to one per household and not valid to present subscribers, expires June 30, 1984. Prices subject to change. Specific titles subject to availability. Allow a minimum of 4 weeks for delivery.

RAPTURE ROMANCE

Provocative and sensual,
passionate and tender—
the magic and mystery of love
in all its many guises

Coming next month

DELINQUENT DESIRE by Carla Neggers. Meeting at a summer camp for delinquent girls, it was unlikely that cool executive Casey Gray and Hollywood agent Jeff Coldwell would give themselves to each other so freely, so passionately. Both shared an unusual secret in their pasts, but by the time the secrets were revealed, it was too late—Casey had lost her cool . . . and her heart. . . .

A SECURE ARRANGEMENT by JoAnn Robb. Jillian Tara Kennedy wasn't prepared for aggressive, seductive Travis Tyrell, who awakened a passion within her she couldn't deny. And even though she'd sworn never to be dependent on any man, Travis' silky caresses broke down her resistance, until she was fighting not his desire, but her own. . . .

ON WINGS OF DESIRE by Jillian Roth. Alaskan bush pilot Erinne Parker was intrigued by mysterious biologist Jansen Lancaster. But being swept into a blazing affair with him only confused her more, and made her wonder if she was learning to love him . . . only to have him leave her. . . .

LADY IN FLIGHT by Diana Morgan. At his first touch, sculptor Sabrina Melendey knew her heart belonged totally to scientist Colin Forrester. But they were as far apart as art and science, and Sabrina didn't believe that love could conquer all. . . .

RAPTURE ROMANCE

Provocative and sensual,
passionate and tender—
the magic and mystery of love
in all its many guises

New Titles Available Now

(0451)

#65 ☐ **WISH ON A STAR by Katherine Ransom.** Fighting for independence from her rich, domineering father, Vanessa Hamilton fled to Maine—and into the arms of Rory McGee. Drawn to his strong masculinity, his sensuous kisses ignited her soul. But she had only just tasted her new-found freedom—was she willing to give herself to another forceful man?
(129083—$1.95)*

#66 ☐ **FLIGHT OF FANCY by Maggie Osborne.** A plane crash brought Samantha Adams and Luke Bannister together for a short, passionate time. But they were rivals in the air freight business, and even though Luke said he loved her and wanted to marry her, Samantha was unsure. Did Luke really want her—or was he only after Adams Air Freight? (128702—$1.95)*

#67 ☐ **ENCHANTED ENCORE by Rosalynn Carroll.** Vicki Owens couldn't resist Patrick Wallingford's fiery embrace years ago, and now he was back reawakening a tantalizing ecstasy. Could she believe love was forever the second time around, or was he only using her to make another woman jealous?
(128710—$1.95)*

#68 ☐ **A PUBLIC AFFAIR by Eleanor Frost.** Barbara Danbury told herself not to trust rising political star Morgan Newman. But she was lost when he pledged his love to her in a night of passion. Then scandal shattered Morgan's ideal image and suddenly Barbara doubted everything—except her burning hunger for him. . . . (128729—$1.95)*

*Price is $2.25 in Canada
To order, use the convenient coupon on the last page.

RAPTURE ROMANCE

Provocative and sensual, passionate and tender— the magic and mystery of love in all its many guises

RAPTURE ROMANCE

*Provocative and sensual,
passionate and tender—
the magic and mystery of love
in all its many guises*

Buy them at your local

bookstore or use coupon

on next page for ordering.